THE CRIME
OF THE
CENTURY

THE CRIME OF THE CENTURY

KINGSLEY AMIS

THE MYSTERIOUS PRESS

New York • London
Tokyo • Sweden • Milan

This work was first published in England by Century Hutchinson Publishing Ltd. and The Sunday Times.

Copyright © 1975 by Kingsley Amis
Alternative Solution copyright © 1975 by Times Newspapers Ltd.

 The Mysterious Press, 129 West 56th Street, New York, N.Y. 10019

Printed in the United States of America
First U.S.A. printing: October 1989
10 9 8 7 6 5 4 3 2 1

Library of Congress Cataloging-in-Publication Data

Amis, Kingsley.
    The crime of the century / Kingsley Amis; intorduced by the author; with
an alternative solution by Howard Martin.
        p.
    "This work was first published in England by Century Hutchinson
Publishing Ltd. and the Sunday Times"—T.p. verso.
    ISBN 0-89296-398-0
    I. Title.
PR6001.M6C74   1989
823'.914--dc20   89-42601
                                                                        CIP

INTRODUCTION

I wrote this summer-holiday serial for a number of reasons. First of all, *The Sunday Times** asked me to. The fee they offered would, I thought, do something to placate my bank manager, whose habitual whinings had lately begun to take on a nasty snarling note. And then I thought it would be a breeze, a dawdle, requiring no more serious effort than that of deciding which weekend to set aside for it.

I was wrong about that, of course. Once again I had forgotten the inescapable truth that there are only two sorts of literary task, the sort you know will give you a lot of trouble and turns out to do just that, and the sort you think you can sail through and turns out to give you a lot of trouble. Some writers never really learn the lesson however often and painfully it may be repeated, like the cheque-bouncer who keeps telling himself that *this* time he will get away with it. I myself have fallen into the same mildly psychopathic error at least twice since, once over compiling a book of quizzes about drink and then again with choosing and introducing a daily poem for a popular newspaper. Yes, I agree heartily that it sounds like money for old rope.

But no accumulation of such reasons would have been enough to get me moving in any of these cases, certainly not on a sustained effort like this serial. Though a great and healthy driving force, the prospect of money needs supercharging with some degree of excitement or enthusiasm or at any rate a desire to take on this specific job and for the moment no other. And I happened to be able to provide that.

According to me, all writing is and should be to some extent a process of imitation: you like reading, you read a lot in general, you find yourself attracted to a particular kind of subdivision of literature, you read that kind intensively, you reach a stage where you begin to think perhaps you can contribute something of that kind yourself. That is probably what is meant by a tradition; it was certainly what got me started on writing in the distant past.

The reading on which my writing has been founded was always various, even indiscriminate, including as it did and taking seriously not only "straight" novels but adventure stories, ghost stories, spy stories, detective stories, science fiction. (I missed the Western, or rather confined my interest in it to the cinema.) By 1975 I had made some sort of contribution to all these genres, and more to the purpose I had recently (1973) published a detective novel, one of a particular type. It had a period, inter-war setting, a complicated method of murder, a great-detective figure with eccentricities, including an obsession with jazz, and plenty of clues and misdirections on the classic model. It was also appropriately domestic, small-scale, involving a limited local community. When the serial was suggested there seemed to be a perfect opportunity for me to have a go at the opposite type of detective story, the one with large thriller or action elements and large forces involved—half Scotland Yard, hundreds of coppers, top political and professional brass, the whole nation holding its breath and the whole of London scared stiff as a mass-murderer prepares to strike again for some unknown but vast and terrible purpose—the crime of the century, in fact. And writing a serial of any sort was something else I had never done before.

As in other kinds of fiction, and not only fiction, an important part of the writer's strategy is to highlight what he thinks he knows about or is good at or anyway is interested in, and to bury or somehow get round the awful gaps in his abilities and stock of information. So here I made the most of my fascinated but amateur acquaintance with forensic psychiatry and my thorough grounding in detective stories. The one had a big say in establishing who might be and who could not be the master-criminal; the other was responsible for the rather heavy doses of inbred stuff about a series of "real" crimes that seemed to be developing along "fictitious" lines. Happily, though, I was able to build this into the plot and the solution in such a way as to make it an essential guide to the identity of the villain and to the reason why he operated as he did.

What I had to conceal as best I could was my state of total inexpertness about anything that might be called police procedure, a field where my chief sources were foggy memories of novels by Agatha Christie and John Dickson Carr and more recent glances at "Z Cars" and other then current TV sagas. In retrospect I can see I was helped by the comparatively undeveloped state of common knowledge of the subject at the time. Even as recently as 12 years ago it was still just possible to seem to cover these matters without a research degree in them, and indeed to tackle any such topic unqualified by diplomas in applied ballistics, nuclear physics, computer science and the rest. Effrontery, that great unsung standby of every sort of novelist, the amiable implication that only a disastrously literal-minded type would insist on a detailed setting-out of the general picture so wittily hinted at, came to the rescue. At least nobody made any objections on that score, then or later.

To rephrase the position only slightly: the novelist is in the business of (among other things) getting away with pretending to know everything about what he only dimly and partially apprehends, and to know enough for his purposes about what he could never even begin to imagine. The procedure is known in the trade as the tip-of-the-iceberg con. I found writing *The Crime of the Century* a most valuable piece of training or refresher course in the basic fictional skills.

More specifically, the gymnasium of the exercise took many pounds of superfluous stylistic flesh off me. The requirements of the format meant that I had to pour an immense amount of detail about suspects, their motivation, their movements, the ways in which their activities might or might not fit in with those of other characters and recent turns of the plot—all that—into an immovably restricted area of point. That in turn meant cutting the whole issue down to the bone, characterisations, descriptions of places and journeys, inner thoughts, any kind of feeling, whatever might be called extra. Well, being forced to dramatise absolutely everything must be good discipline for—here we go again—any kind of novelist.

When I look back now on the result, on what I actually wrote, my reactions are patchy, though not much more so than to any of my other finished products. Indeed I still cherish the verdict of the great Julian Symons that the working-out of the plot here, the actual detection, was reasonably watertight, something he had regretted not being able to say of *The Riverside Villas Murder*, my full-dress crime novel. I seem to remember he went so far as to commend the method used to pick up the ransom or blackmail payment under the noses of the police. To be honest, I thought it was not too bad myself.

A couple of other minor riddles give me some slight cause for complacency; I mention them briefly now to give the reader a hand in solving what I will admit is a pretty thorny puzzle. One is the reason why somebody who could have named the arch-criminal, and had a strong motive for doing so, didn't. The remaining point concerns the character Christopher Dane—a jolly handy invention of mine, by the way, bringing with him what as far as I know is an original method of misdirecting the inquisitive reader. The extract from his current novel right at the beginning of the text is there to set going the apparent coincidence of the plot of that novel with the series of "real" murders starting at the same time, sure, and further to establish just for fun what a lousy writer he is. But it also conceals a hefty clue to the perpetrator of those murders.

Kingsley Amis

The Crime of the Century was published between 13 July and 28 September 1975. After Episode 5 readers were invited to send in their own solutions: the winning entry by Howard Martin is published for the first time in book form alongside Kingsley Amis's own (and completely different) denouement.

THE CRIME
OF THE
CENTURY

CHAPTER ONE

"Some people are never satisfied," Fenton said meaningfully. "They get to be famous or they pile up a mountain of cash and then they find that wasn't what they wanted after all."

Porter scratched his grizzled head. "I don't quite see how that applies to our man, sir."

"Ah, but we're not necessarily thinking of the same man. Who's your candidate, Sir Oliver?"

The famous industrialist gave Fenton a sharp look but his tone was mild when he answered: "Oh, I've no views, James. Detection isn't in my line. I leave that to clever fellows like you and professionals like the Super here."

As he spoke the car rounded a curve. Began to slow down. Stopped at the roadside amid a jumble of vehicles and men in uniform. Also a couple of men in civilian clothes. Fenton, the Superintendent and after a moment Sir Oliver Trefusis got out of the car. The sky was thick

1

with cloud, more rain on the way. An inspector saluted, said: "You'll be wanting to see the doctor, gentlemen."

That individual, a balding bustling man around forty, said: "Died some time between midnight and dawn. I can't be more definite before the autopsy. Killed in the same way as the others. No sexual interference."

"We're dealing with a maniac," Porter said.

"I beg to differ," Fenton said quietly.

Christopher Dane read through the lines of his typescript and gave a gentle groan. A moment later, the famous industrialist had been demoted to a merely well-known one and had got out of the car at the same time as Fenton and the Superintendent. After all, all three remained in suspended animation while Dane got up from his work-table and paced the floor. He resembled his fictional doctor in being "around" forty, but his mop of reddish hair showed no signs of thinning and he had never bustled in his life.

The front-door buzzer sounded from the hall of the flat. Dane went out to the intercom.

"Yes?"

"It's me," said a steady feminine voice.

A short time afterwards, the owner of the voice was in the kitchen unloading groceries from a supermarket bag. Rosemary Dane, a long-legged dark blonde in her thirties, had not yet that day set eyes on her husband. This was customary. It was part of a much larger custom whereby, twice a year, he took rooms near their house in Hamilton Terrace and moved into them for a couple of weeks to do nothing else but eat, sleep and write a new

James Fenton mystery. Some of Rosemary's friends had queried that "nothing else" from time to time, but not to her face, and she herself never did, nor had she felt the need to do so. Fenton could not emerge effectively, the pair of them had proved, unless there were no children about, no visitors, no telephone, no mail and that was that.

The kitchen had been cleared up by the daily woman, who had seen Dane for a full thirty seconds the previous day, his first in residence, and might well have a similar experience on his last. Rosemary moved into the quite large and not very uncomfortable sitting-room, where the central heating was more than coping with the December cold. She put down on the sofa the current *Evening Chronicle,* an intruder tolerated purely for its crime reports, and waited.

Dane finished a sentence at the typewriter, came over and hugged her warmly yet absentmindedly.

"Everything all right?" he asked.

"Fine."

"What a dear little thing you are, in spite of being so tall."

"It's a feat, isn't it?"

After a pause, Dane released his wife, moved away and stared into space. Many women in this situation would have asked something like: "How's it going?" Rosemary did not, and never had; Dane often said it was the best single non-physical thing about her. Now, after more staring, he said:

"It's not going too well."

"Oh?"

"This bloody playing by the rules. Early mention of the criminal, so that roughly if it were a serial he'd have to come into the first installment—no real problem as long as it need only be a mention. All clues shared with the reader—if you can think of some. Sit down a minute. No vital coincidences—you can do quite a bit with non-vital ones. No secret passages, poisons unknown to science, twin brothers—yes, yes, yes. The really boring one is never being allowed to show what's in the criminal's mind even when it's nothing to do with the crime. You have to plug away with twitching mouths and fleeting expressions and . . . sharp looks."

"Agatha Christie showed a hell of a lot of what was in the criminal's mind in *The Murder of Roger Ackroyd*."

"That was in 1926. And Agatha's a law unto herself. I'm seriously thinking of chucking it in. That rule, I mean."

"I'd seriously think again about that. The Fenton fans would be certain to—"

"How many of those precious Fenton fans would notice the difference?"

"I've no idea," said Rosemary from the sofa. "But the reviewers would, and they'd stop calling Dane the last of the classic detective writers, which is one of your big selling-points. Surely."

"Mm." After circling the room, hands in pockets, Dane had come to where his wife was sitting. His glance fell to the newspaper, which he picked up with an uncharacteristically quick movement and began to read attentively.

Neither spoke for a time. Outside, a heavy lorry made

a thunderous gear-change, rattling the windows of the room.

"It's much noisier here than that place you took in the summer," said Rosemary as a reminder of her presence.

"A noise you can't do anything about doesn't count as a noise," said her husband without lifting his eyes from the print, then went on, evidently quoting, "A police spokesman stated this morning that there were some unusual features about the case which would be revealed at the proper time."

"Is that the girl on the common?"

"Yes. What unusual features? What proper time?"

"Raped, was she? I only glanced at it."

"No sexual interference."

"Why the fascination?"

"I hope they catch him, of course." Dane lowered the paper, but his eyes were still on it. "There's something horribly attractive about real crime which you just don't get at all in fictional crime. No way of doing it. A totally different kind of thrill."

"Is 'attractive' the word?"

"It isn't only nice things that attract people. We'd all have a much better time if it were different, I agree. Would we? I don't know. You'd better clear off, pet."

"All right, darling—see you tomorrow."

The newspaper report that had interested Christopher Dane had had a similar effect on a certain Henry Addams at an address in Bow, more marked, perhaps: it certainly took a more practical and laborious form. Addams, a small but strongly built person in his fifties, grey-haired

and bespectacled, read the report over his evening meal,
to which he had sat down immediately upon arriving
home just before six o'clock. After putting down his final
cup of tea, he rose to his feet with decision and said to his
wife:

"I think I'll go over to the study for a bit, dear."

"All right, dear. Will you be back for 'Coronation
Street'?"

"I'll see," said Addams in his thin voice.

Taking with him the paper, and also a stiff-cover
exercise book bought that day in his lunch-break, he left
the house by the back door, crossed the strip of garden
and unlocked the door of a prefabricated hut he had
assembled himself some years previously. This was what
he called his study; what he did in it he called working
with his books. Once inside, he relocked the door, which
was never unlocked except to allow him to enter and
leave. The interior was sparely but adequately furnished:
a deal table, a battered chest of drawers serving as a kind
of filing cabinet, a hard chair with a cushion on it, an
easy chair, a two-bar electric fire. Thanks to this, and to
the careful insulation of the door-frame and the two
permanently shuttered windows, the place was comfortably warm in a few minutes.

Addams sat down at the table on the hard chair. With
unhurried, precise movements he used a razor-blade and
a steel rule to cut from the newspaper the report he had
read earlier. Just as neatly, he gummed the clipping to
the third page of the exercise-book (the first two would
be needed for entering the contents) and added the date
in a small upright hand. This done, he took from a shelf

a well-thumbed volume called *Compendium of Blood*, settled down with it in the easy chair, and turned to the chapter on Peter Kürten, the Düsseldorf sadist, arsonist and mass murderer. Henry Addams was soon happily absorbed.

Among the thousands of other people in London who read the report with particular care, five more might be mentioned. Four of them were unknown except in certain specialised quarters: Lucian Toye (as he was sometimes known), a highly qualified doctor, a devoted reader of Dane's James Fenton mysteries and a life-long misogynist; Evan Williams, a Post Office worker lately released after six years in a psychiatric hospital; Ronnie Grainger, a garage employee released about the same time after four years in prison for assault with a deadly weapon, his second offence under that charge; and Arthur Johnson, a watchmaker's assistant with an unreciprocated passion for a girl named Tessa Noble, a barmaid at his local pub.

The name of the fifth man was known throughout his profession and beyond. Sir Neil Costello, QC, had the previous months added a further legal triumph to an impressive record by securing the conviction of a murderer who, to all appearances, had been as innocent as the man in the moon. Costello had treated his colleagues' congratulations with reserve. He had maintained (so rumour said) that the old-fashioned criminal lawyer had lost any significance he might once have had, with acts of terrorism replacing the traditional privately motivated murder as a focus of public interest, and that it would be interesting to see if even a career like that of Jack the

Ripper would nowadays cause more than local concern.

It was far less widely known that Lady Costello, wife of Sir Neil, was an alcoholic.

Costello himself was a moderate, social drinker. That evening, in the bar of the Irving Club near Trafalgar Square, his tipple was chilled white wine. With his great height and abundant white hair, he stood out among the small group of members near the massive Edwardian fireplace. The talk—not surprisingly, since the combined ages of the four easily topped two hundred—was of "youth" and its ways.

The most eloquent was the Under-Secretary of State at the Ministry of Domestic Affairs, Dickie Lambert-Syme. If Costello could be called a caricature of a distinguished barrister, Lambert-Syme was equally a caricature of what a man so named ought not to look like: built like a heavyweight boxer but now running to fat, nearly bald head and heavy beard showing beneath the skin. With a favourite gesture, always used by the many people who did imitations of him, he banged his right fist into his left palm and growled.

"There are only two sorts—the bloody little fools and the rotten little swine. Both sexes. I deal with them every day. And every day I thank my lucky stars I'm not married."

"My three don't seem too bad," murmured George Henderson, the shortest and thinnest of the group, a physique possibly earned by a lifetime of devoted cigarette-smoking.

"Give them their daily fix of Benedict Royal and they're perfectly happy."

"Oh, God." Quintin Young's handsome, lined face twisted into a passable tragic mask.

"Same with my two. Is he actually trying to make the most horrible noises anybody could think of or is that just the way it comes out?"

"Who is this Royal person?" asked Costello.

"Now then, Neil, you're not a judge yet," said Lambert-Syme good-humouredly.

"Benedict Royal is a very, perhaps I should say an excessively well known pop singer. And I'm not going to tell you what a pop singer is. I quite agree with Quintin about the noises he makes, but in fact—you're not going to like this—he's not a bad bloke."

"Oh yes he is," said Young. "He must be. It stands to reason."

"Have you ever met him?"

"He wouldn't be alive now if I had."

Lambert-Syme showed his huge teeth in a grin. "You of all people ought to know better than to go by appearance, Quintin. All that capering and yelling and the rest of it is just part of the act. When you talk to him he's quiet, behaves like a human being, bit over-dressed by our standards, sure, but . . . He's bright, too—does *The Times* crossword in fifteen minutes, if that's any guide. And I'll tell you something else between the four of us. He's helped us more than once at the Ministry."

"Like you're joking, man," said Henderson.

"Never more serious in my life, George. He gets around, you see. Knows about all sorts of places and people that don't exist for any of us. For instance, he hates drugs and at the same time he hears things about

where they come from. He had a hand in that big police
haul in Knightsbridge a couple of months ago. And you
probably remember we got the chaps who did the bomb
at the Brazilian joint. We wouldn't have without young
Royal."

Costello spoke in the mildly amazed pause. "Talking of
persons who may or may not be horrible, or deemed
horrible, I'm expecting Fergus MacBean any minute, so
consider yourselves warned."

"I deem him horrible," said Young, "but if I may I'll
stay around for a few minutes just to have a look at him."

"Don't you deem him off his rocker as well?" asked
Henderson.

"No, just horrible. That's quite enough, though."

"Indeed."

"Can't stand the chap myself." Lambert-Syme looked
at the watch on his hairy wrist. "Got to be off in a minute
anyway—little champagne-party for two. Yes, he's a
pain in the neck to us."

"I can't imagine what you want with him, Neil," said
Young. "I should have thought you'd have had enough of
him on that committee of his."

"I did, hence my resignation from it. But it's he that
wants something with me. I suggested he came here so
that at least I'd be on friendly territory. And I see he's
come here. Now's your chance to slip away, Dickie."

Lambert-Syme made off in a wide sweep that took him
well clear of the approaching figure. The Right Honour-
able Fergus MacBean, MP, would not have looked
horrible to most observers; tall, square-shouldered, with
fair hair brushed up from the brow, he was of attractive,

if slightly effeminate, appearance. What so many people deemed horrible about him was his views, or rather his view, incessantly urged: that every kind of convicted criminal should have a much worse time than at present, with the rope for murderers, castration for habitual sex offenders, prolonged solitary confinement for prison rioters, though not (to Costello's expressed surprise) amputation of the right hand for thieves. On all other matters he was an impeccable moderate, even liberal: satisfied with the state of the law regarding homosexuality, not specially concerned either way about pornography, positively hostile to racial discrimination—that last was a sore point for those of his fellow-MPs whose constituencies lay in urban trouble-spots while MacBean sat safely for a West of England agricultural area.

Costello introduced him, saying, "I don't think you know Quintin Young and George Henderson."

"By repute only." MacBean gave a warm smile and shook hands in turn in a slightly Germanic fashion. "Dr. Young. Dr. Henderson. Do say at once, either or both of you, if you've already put me down as a dangerous psychopath and/or a man on the immediate brink of a cerebral haemorrhage."

Among the three of them, the others managed a quite creditable burst of laughter. Costello went off to the bar. MacBean smiled again and said in his soft but clear voice, slightly marked by a Lanarkshire accent:

"Well, gentlemen, another wanton murder today, or yesterday rather: the stabbing in Barn Elms Park. You've probably laid bets I'd introduce the topic, but I'll go ahead regardless. The question's too important. Here's

this young girl been made away with in circumstances
that hardly seem to suggest a family quarrel or a brawl in
a bar or even robbery. Let's assume, at any rate, that this
killing was premeditated. Would we be safe in assuming
with total certainty that, were the death penalty for
murder in force in the land, that consideration would
have no deterrent effect whatever on any mental or
emotional type of person? It's scarcely a new point, but
it's not every day I meet a distinguished forensic psychiatrist, so I hope you'll forgive me if I ask you for your
professional opinion."

Young sighed quietly. (Henderson had often heard
him say how much he hated such interrogations outside
working hours.) "Well, to begin with, *total* certainty on
any matter concerning the mind is inconceivable . . ."

"I think that to concede so much concedes an all-
important part of my case, Dr. Young—it would be false
modesty on my part not to assume that you know well
enough what my case is."

"Yes, I do. And it probably does. The concession you
mentioned." Young gave a mildly despairing glance over
at Costello, still waiting his turn at the crowded bar.

"If I may say so, I suggest you should not allow the
matter to rest there. Assuming you do in fact concede my
point, you ought to lend your name, with the weight it
carries, to the work I'm trying to do."

"With what object? I don't see—"

"Let's start," said MacBean pleasantly, also with the air
of starting something that would go on for quite a long
time, "by considering the people whose business it is to
control crime and criminals: the police. Their knowledge

that an apprehended murderer, instead of suffering his deserts, will be at large again within a few years is, my inquiries suggest, a substantial disincentive and discouragement to the detection forces. Their morale is low . . ."

Morale was certainly not high in the Murder Room at the headquarters of the Regional Crime Squad concerned with the Barn Elms Park killing. The officer in charge of the Squad, Detective-Superintendent Victor Ware, entered to find the officer in charge of the case, Detective-Inspector John Kemp, apparently in silent communion with his assistant, Detective-Sergeant Roger Masterton. The trestle table between them was littered with sheaves of typescripts and bundles of photographs.

"Sorry, I'm late," said Ware, striding in on short legs, then added, "but I can see I'd only have been in everybody's way. Where you fellows get all this . . . crackling energy from beats me hollow."

Kemp nodded his large dark head. "Yes, I could see how it would, sir. But we'd need more than energy to make any progress tonight. Or ever, possibly."

"What have you got?"

"That won't take long. Sergeant."

"I want it in full." Ware lit a cigarette with an angry movement.

"It still won't take long, sir. Sergeant."

"Bridget Ainsworth, sir," said Masterton. "Twenty. Stabbed five times in the back with an unusually thin blade: that's the autopsy—there was nothing there, at the scene that is. No assault. No theft. No evidence she put up a struggle: nothing under her fingernails or any of that. No extraneous hairs or fibres on her clothing. Her parents say she said she was going to the movies locally, walking distance. None of the cinema staff remember her. Found near the road by a motorist just after seven A.M.; saw her lying there. The place is a couple of miles from her route to the cinema and back. Time of death, hour or two either side of midnight. Consistent with her going to the film, given a lift on her way home, stabbed in the car and dumped. Quiet girl, respectable, one steady boy-friend, also respectable, not that that matters one way or the other because he was in bed with 'flu at the time, which was why he didn't take her to the cinema, lives with his parents and his mother looked in on him a couple of times late on to see he was all right. Popular at work, that's the girl, but no close friends. I can give you names if you want, sir, but I thought—"

"No, that's enough for now, thank you," said Ware. "Well, what you've got seems to consist mainly of what you haven't got."

Kemp nodded again.

"There's a bit more of what we haven't got. No prospect of any material witness. No prospect of finding the weapon: this chap's obviously too fly for that."

"You mean the nothing on the clothing. What did he do, swathe himself in plastic? Where's the Scotch?"

"Sergeant. . . . And the thin blade."

"No blood on him."

"Very little on her, come to that. Repeated stabbing not because he was in a frenzy."

"Because he hadn't got the medical knowledge to make sure of getting a vital spot first time."

"Or because he'd got the medical knowledge that would tell him just getting one vital spot may not be immediately fatal with a thin blade."

"You know too bloody much, Kemp."

"Only what the doc told me, sir."

"Mm." Ware took his Scotch and tap-water from Masterton, gazing in apparent wonder at the cracked and smeared tooth-glass containing it. "Thanks. Cheers. Any more noes?"

"One or two, yes. No footprints, or a thousand footprints: the ground's hard. Similarly, no handy patch of mud for tyre-tracks, not that they're ever any help. But there is just one thing, which I've been holding back until now for dramatic effect."

Ware took the leaf of slippery paper. "Where's the original?"

"Still out. But it's the *Evening Chronicle.*"

"Well, it wouldn't be the *Budleigh Salterton Advertiser*, would it? And 'S' and a thing that might be half an 'O' or most of a 'C.' Or a 'G.'"

"They reckon it's an 'O,' sir. Pinned to the lapel of her topcoat. And there's another no there too, of course. No prints."

"Naturally not."

"Final no—no suggestions."

"Sergeant?"

"More Scotch, sir?"

"No, you fool. I mean not yet, thank you. Does 'SO' mean anything to you?"

"Part of a longer word, sir?"

"Mm." Ware stretched his ill-proportioned frame. "I'm afraid you may be right. Can I see a picture? Her face?"

Kemp reached across again. "Nothing much there," he said.

"If anything, mild surprise."

"You might be mildly surprised if someone . . ."

"I can't see any fear. But I'm frightened myself. I don't know why, but I am."

"Really?"

"You don't reckon on getting anything from the appeals."

"No, sir, I don't. We'd need something not far short of a car number, and you get that kind of thing straight away or not at all."

"There's always a first time. But I agree . . . You'd better just take me quickly through the medical report and the parents' statement and the . . ."

While Kemp turned over the typescripts, Ware signalled for, and was poured, more to drink. He said casually to Kemp. "How's your mother-in-law?"

"On the mend, I gather, but Mary's still with her."

"And the kids?"

"They're there too, of course."

"So you're on your own."

"Yes, why?"

"Ah, here we are . . . five foot six . . . average physique . . . not a virgin. You didn't mention that."

"I'm sorry, sir, I assumed you'd assume it. If it'd been the other way round I'd have mentioned it. After all, she was 20, not 12."

"Getting a little heated, aren't we?"

"Well, sir, you see my daughter's 12."

"And you still say he's not off his rocker," said Henderson to Young. "After the way he went on at poor old Neil all through their dinner. No wonder it packed up so early."

"He could be off his rocker, of course, like all sorts of people you pass in the street who aren't actually frothing at the mouth. I'm only saying I see no sign of it so far."

"The fellow's a monomaniac."

"Now come on, George, even a mere wielder of the knife like you must know that that's a journalistic myth. Was Beethoven a monomaniac about music? This chap could be nothing more than a careerist, and they aren't mad. Not necessarily, anyway. Let's polish off that port."

The two old friends—they had met in their first year at medical school and had kept in close touch while Young climbed to the top of his chosen tree in psychiatry, Henderson likewise in surgery—were lounging in a corner of the Irving Club coffee-room under a large full-length portrait of its patron in the part of Richard III. Earlier, they had eaten together at the common table in the dining-room, well placed, by chance, to observe the private table where the QC and the MP had been sitting. The doctors' conversation, after a long tour among insane psychiatrists and alcoholic surgeons, had just reverted to Fergus MacBean.

"I can't bear the way he smiles all the time," pursued Henderson.

"I know."

"It's out of key with what he's talking about. Haven't I heard you say that that sort of thing is characteristic of schizophrenics?"

"If he described a hanging in detail, with gusts of merriment at intervals, it wouldn't look too good, agreed. No, he just realises, very sanely, that a lot of chaps will think he must be some sort of monster to hold those views of his, and he wants to show that he's really terrifically human, warm, decent et cetera."

"Maybe. To hell with him, anyhow. We'd better be off before they lock us in. Hey, I ran into an old pal of yours the other day. Marcus Varga."

"Oh, God." Young's expression left it open whether he was about to spit or to cry. "That idiot. Now he really is mad."

"You mean it?"

"Most certainly I mean it, and you can quote me. All that sociometrical lot are mad, apart from the ones that are just bloody fools, and Varga's very bright, I'm sorry to say. How did you run into him?"

"Some dinner at the . . ."

Henderson's voice stopped as if a gramophone needle had been taken off a record. They had reached the hall of the club, buttoning their overcoats, and Henderson had glanced at the teleprinter there, an amenity popular with members of financial or sporting interests.

"What . . . ?"

Young looked over his friend's shoulder and read:

23.45 BODY OF UNIDENTIFIED GIRL AGED AROUND 20 FOUND HAMMER-SMITH PARK SHEPHERD'S BUSH. CAUSE OF DEATH MULTIPLE STAB WOUNDS. POLICE BELIEVE LINKED WITH STAB VICTIM BRIDGET AINSWORTH FOUND EARLY THIS A.M. ENDS.

"Well, there's a coincidence," said Henderson.

"Eh?"

"After what we were talking about a couple of hours ago."

"Actually it was nearly five hours ago," said Young. "Not that it matters."

A little later that night, Sir Neil Costello let himself into his house in Eaton Square and went to his study on the ground floor. As a result of diligent practice, his progress was completely noiseless, nor was there a sound when he unlocked a drawer in his desk and a moment later locked it again. After the same fashion, his steps guided by the electric torch he had switched on after shutting the front door, he made his way to his dressing-room on the first floor. Here he turned on the light, put the switched-off torch in a drawer (left unlocked this time), washed his hands carefully and changed into pyjamas. All his movements were unhurried to the point of extreme relaxation. His expression, similarly, was more than calm: it would not have taken Quintin Young's training to see in it something beyond simple fatigue, a look, perhaps, the recent and full satisfaction of an urgent desire. But, of course, there was no one there to see any of that.

There was no one to see in the bedroom either; the person already there was in no condition to do much seeing. Olivia Costello's slow, deep breathing did not alter a fraction when her husband put the light on, looked at her face with its loose jowls and open mouth, looked away, slipped into bed and extinguished the light. Once in bed and asleep she seldom woke, but there had been occasions when her fourteen or fifteen hours' drinking had laid her out on the drawing-room sofa, in the bathroom, on the bedroom floor, and discomfort had roused her. In such a case, even her blurred brain could have been relied on to register the difference between her husband's presence and his absence, but Costello had made full preparation to deal with that contingency.

At about the same time Benedict Royal was taking a late drink in his Regent's Park mansion. With him were his manager, Marty Mannheim, and a girl called Karen Priest. A young man who looked like a soccer star in mufti, but was in fact a kind of butler, served them with 12-year-old malt whisky in heavy cut-glass tumblers, and left.

"Who were they?" asked Karen, returning to an earlier theme. "Just give me one name."

Mannheim sighed noisily.

"Can't you see he's tired? To begin with, he was working all the afternoon with the band while you were sitting on your fat—"

"Him being tired doesn't mean you can't tell me who was there, does it? Oh, I know, no use telling me because the names wouldn't mean anything to a slut like me, eh?"

"That's right, never listen. I told you, some of the names would mean plenty to you and if anybody gets to hear they're talking to Benedict and I, then a lot of people could guess what we're talking about and we got to keep that dead quiet. Absolutely essential we keep it dead quiet."

"All blokes, was it, there?"

"Oh no. One female, just the kind he likes to pull. Oh . . . Love, she was fifty, some fellow's secretary, and it was a sort of conference. That's the best way you could understand it. Talking, discussion. A conference. You know."

Karen Priest drew her rather celebrated legs up under her on what looked like the genuine alligator-hide upholstery of the broad couch.

"Suppose they did mean something to me, the names, why shouldn't I get to know them?"

"You'd tell someone," said Royal in a gentle, explanatory tone. "Whether you knew what you were doing or not, a chat would happen and the word would get filtered around and something worth something and a row of noughts would end up dead. You'd tell someone. I'm moving along. Bring me the book in ten minutes, Marty?"

"Yes, Benedict."

Mannheim turned to Karen and spoke to her urgently in a lower tone. Royal gave no sign of retiring; instead, he stabbed with his fingers at a console beside his velvet-covered armchair. A television screen sparkled and sizzled for a moment, then, without pause or preliminary, the top half of a man appeared and said:

"The body of 19-year-old Elizabeth Buck was found earlier tonight in Hammersmith Park, within a short distance of the BBC television centre. She had been repeatedly stabbed. Miss Buck was not an employee of the BBC and her home was in Bethnal Green. Her parents had no other children. Now the weather:"—an abrupt change of key—"and it's overcoats and mittens again, sorry. Frost in—"

A click, then silence. Mannheim's face showed mild surprise and shock, either genuine or very expertly assumed. Karen gave no sign of having heard. Royal leaned forward with a jerk and slammed his glass down on a marble table with enough force to have broken a less sturdy vessel.

"Bastard," he said, still with a kind of gentleness. "We'll have to get him. Fast."

"How do you mean, we?" Karen sounded cross, but little more so than usual.

"I mean me."

"You and whose army?"

"I know people. I can do something. There must be something I can do."

"You coming to bed?"

"Not now, not for a bit. I'll see the book in the morning, Marty."

CHAPTER TWO

"We're dealing with a maniac," Porter said.

"I beg to differ," Fenton said quietly.

Fenton had said nothing more, done nothing more, for nearly thirty-six hours. On the evening after the second murder, Christopher Dane sat staring at his typescript. Never before, once started on a new book, had he failed to write a single line for such a period. When she visited him that morning, however, his wife had found him in apparent good spirits, implying by his manner, although not stating, that his difficulties of the previous day were solved.

That afternoon he had walked down to the shopping centre and walked back carrying a portable TV set: another break with custom, for television stood alongside the telephone and not out of sight behind the children as one of the distractions that drove him from home at these times. The set stood now within his reach. On its screen a girl was holding up a packet of washing-powder and no doubt lauding its contents, though, with the sound turned right down as it was, this had to be inferred from the nature of things backed up by the intensity of her gestures. After a moment of seeming paralysis, she vanished, and a stylised likeness of the Palace of Westminster came into view, followed by a title, CRIME TEN. Dane turned up the sound as a dark-haired man with spectacles—identified by a caption as one Wells Richman—began to speak. After a preliminary or two, he said:

"The most shocking events of the week have undoubtedly been the fatal stabbings of Bridget Ainsworth and Elizabeth Buck. The police are anxious to trace their movements just before they died. First, Bridget Ainsworth. . . ."

Richman went on to show photographs and film relevant to the two cases, asked for information, gave telephone numbers. Then the camera closed on some sort of knife, one with an unusually long, thin and narrow blade.

"This isn't the murder weapon, which has yet to be found: it's a replica prepared by forensic experts. There's no proper hilt on it because nothing is known about the hilt on the actual weapon. But if you've sold a knife with a blade like this to anybody, or if you've seen one in anybody's possession, the police would be glad to hear from you. Now"—another close-up—"these pieces cut out of a newspaper were found pinned to the victims' clothing. S O U. It doesn't seem to mean much, does it? But if you've noticed anyone cutting up a newspaper in this sort of way, or come across a newspaper with small pieces cut out, let the police know. As always, your information will be treated in the strictest confidence. Finally, be careful. Don't go out alone after dark. Don't accept lifts from strangers. This applies to everyone, but particularly, of course, young girls. If you have to go out on your own, stay where the crowds are. The police believe more crimes of this sort may be on the way.

"Now the furniture warehouse robbery in Shoreditch. At about 10 A.M.—"

Henry Addams got up briskly from his television chair (he had provided it with a hinged flap to accommodate snacks his wife brought him), took from the mantelpiece the long cardboard tube he had brought home that day, and made for the sitting-room door.

"Aren't you going to stay for the news, dear?"

"I won't bother, dear. I've got some work to do with my books. I may be late, so don't wait up."

"All right, dear."

Mrs. Addams was quite incurious about what that work with the books was, and equally so about the strength of her husband's devotion to it. When, as had happened a couple of times in the past, she had awoken in the small hours and found him absent from her side, she had at once accepted his explanation later that he had had an unusually important piece of work to finish. Now she fetched the cushion-cover she was embroidering and settled down to her own work.

In his study down the garden, Addams brought his new scrap-book up to date. This done, he opened the cardboard cylinder, pulled out a large map of Greater London and fixed it to the wall with drawing-pins. Next, carefully and efficiently as ever, he prepared three small paper flags of the type used for indicating the position of military units. What he wrote in tiny script on the first two, however, was nothing to do with tanks or artillery; it was "Bridget Ainsworth" and "Elizabeth Buck." Referring to his scrap-book, Addams inserted them in the appropriate places on the map, contemplated the third flag with a small smile, put it away in the chest of drawers and left the hut, making little noise.

That same evening, three men in a basement room near Kennington Oval sat staring at the just-extinguished screen of a small TV set, similar in pattern to the one Christopher Dane had hired.

The eldest of the three spoke. "They're not really worried yet, are they?" (An expert would have recognized his accent as that of County Fermanagh.)

"They will be tomorrow morning, Sean. And this here won't exactly cheer them up."

"Let me see that again." A sheet of paper passed from one to the other. "Yeah. Yeah. Isn't a hundred thousand a wee bit modest?"

"This is only the first time of asking."

"British Liberation Army. That'll annoy the bastards. Yeah, I like it. It's good. Okay, wrap it up."

"Right."

The man called Sean, who had not touched the paper at any point, looked curiously at the other as he folded it and put it in an envelope. "Listen, aren't you worried about your dabs and your writing at all? They can get that from blocks as well as the ordinary stuff, didn't I tell you?"

"They'll only find out I wrote it if we're caught, and it isn't going to matter then, is it? They don't know me." Another paper went into another envelope. "Not the way they know you."

"To hell, they won't be after me for this caper. Soon as it gets hot the Officials and the Provisionals both'll disclaim responsibility." The Ulsterman turned to the third man in the room. "They know you, though. Doesn't it bother you?"

"Not a bloody toss, my old friend," said Ronnie Grainger. "Form for assault with a deadly weapon? The Russkies'll be landing by the time they get down my way. What bothers me's the pick-up."

"Early days yet, Ron," said the second man. "I've got an idea or two."

"They better be better than the blokes in *Dirty Harry*, pal. Those things ready yet?"

"Here."

Grainger got to his feet, took the sealed, stamped envelopes in a grubby handkerchief and pushed them into his side pocket. Sean ran his eyes over him, grinning slightly.

"Step carefully, now, smiler. We don't want any blood on that nice suit of yours."

"Look, don't get witty. Don't get witty."

"Ah, no offence. Be away with you. We'll see you the morrow."

"We've got to do something," said Charles Paynter, a

small bright-eyed man whose rise in politics had been closely connected with his unwavering lack of fear of the obvious.

Dickie Lambert-Syme stirred his bulk in a chair on the opposite side of the leather-topped desk. "Seem to be doing something, at least. I frankly don't think this committee will get us anywhere, Minister, but I agree it's the only idea so far that makes any kind of political sense."

"Mm. What's your view, Follett?"

"While I'm working, sir, I haven't got a political view, as you know." The other member of the group at one end of the long Whitehall office was Special Commissioner Peter Follett of Scotland Yard, stout, fair-complexioned, with an abundant head of brown hair streaked with grey. "But I'm not altogether pessimistic about the possible usefulness of a committee, probably because it's taking so much out of me not to be altogether pessimistic about the usefulness of orthodox police methods on this case, however intensive, and they're very intensive already. So—let's go ahead as soon as you think would be politically desirable."

"Very well. Who do you want?"

"Bill Barry for a start, sir."

"Hasn't he retired?" asked Lambert-Syme.

"Last year, yes. Which means he can give all his time to this. He knows more about criminal investigation than anybody else. Then I'd like Quintin Young and George Henderson."

Paynter looked honestly puzzled. "I can see why you might think you need a psychiatrist, but from what one

knows at the moment I should have thought a patholo-
gist's services would be . . . inefficacious."

"Quite likely, sir, at the moment, but that may change.
And Henderson's a useful man in a general way. Bright
as hell. I've worked with him before."

"Very well," said the Minister again. "Anybody else?"

"I'd like an ordinary copper, somebody up in the
firing-line, so to speak. This chap Kemp on the
Ainsworth case struck me as pretty sound, with a bit of
imagination thrown in. That's all from me for now."

"Right. Dickie?"

"Well, obviously a legal luminary of some sort. I
should say Neil Costello's as good as any, wouldn't you?"

"And known to the public. Agreed."

"Fergus MacBean."

"Oh dear," said Paynter. "Just imagine what the Press
will do with that."

"I appreciate the point, Minister, but there's the
feeling in the country to be considered." Lambert-Syme
broke into surprisingly efficient loutish diction. "Good
ole Fergy, 'e'll get the sod if anyone can—means business, ole Fergy does." He ended in his normal tones, "It
would help to steady morale."

"Mm . . . yes . . . I'll just have to get the P.M. in a
good mood. Go on."

"Marcus Varga. Appointing him would—"

Commissioner Follett had scowled at the mention of
MacBean, but in silence. Now he said forcefully, "Sir,
are we trying to run a serious criminal inquiry or a
television chat show? What on earth could be the contribution of a clown like Varga?"

"I know what you mean, Peter," cut in Lambert-Syme before the Minister could reply, "but there's a real brain there . . ."

"Well concealed."

". . . and we need someone to offset MacBean. You must see how important it is to present this bunch of—this committee—as an entirely balanced body. If someone gets up in the House—"

Now Paynter cut in. "I don't think we need pursue the point, Dickie. As the Commissioner says, in his official capacity he has no political opinions."

"I'm not trying to be political, sir, just sensible if I can. I want to—"

"Yes, well your objection has been noted and now I'm afraid we must get on. Yes, Dickie?"

"Just a final name, one which may strike you a little far-fetched, Minister, but here goes. Benedict Royal, the pop singer. Now I can foresee opposition, of course. . . ."

Paynter caught sight of the look on Follett's face and said quickly, "Perhaps, but there's no reason why we should let that deter us. Royal has helped us in unofficial ways in the past and I'm sure he'll give of his best this time. Sophisticated tactical move, too. Good thinking, Dickie."

"Thank you, Minister." Lambert-Syme showed relief at having his suggestion so promptly taken up. "I'll set the wheels in motion straight away."

"There's not a moment to be lost," said Paynter with conviction.

                          *   *   *

Marcus Varga was living alone at this time. For reasons
he had not yet divulged to anyone, his fourth wife had
recently left him. Her first and third predecessors had
behaved in much the same way; the second had departed
more thoroughly by taking an overdose of sleeping pills.
The coroner's jury had found insufficient evidence to
ascertain whether this had been accidental or designed;
those who knew Varga had tended to take the second
view, and wondered extremely what it was about him
that induced women to keep marrying him.

    Possibly it was his appearance: tall, emaciated,
evangelical-eyed, his prematurely grey hair at fashion-
able medium length, his clothes tending to velvet jackets,
frilled shirts, floppy bows. He was attired in some such
way, under a corduroy overcoat, as he paid off his taxi
outside the rather vulgar Georgian building that housed
the Ministry of Domestic Affairs.

    A whiskered young man approached. "Dr. Varga?"
"Yes?"

    "Oh, it's Westminster Television, sir. Would you mind
having a few words with our interviewer?"

    "Not at all, but it must be very quick," said Varga in
his thick Hungarian accent, one of those that become
thinner at moments of excitement.

    It was very quick: in less than a minute another young
man was saying, "This is a new departure for you, Dr.
Varga."

    "Yes, and for the others also. Except of course the
police people."

"Er, quite. Tell me, what does it feel like to be taking part in a criminal inquiry?"

"I've no idea. I don't regard this as a criminal inquiry in the true sense."

"But surely—"

"A real criminal inquiry would be asking who are those who have made our society what it is."

"You don't feel hopeful, then, about the prospects of this meeting."

"I feel hopeful about nearly nothing. I came out of curiosity."

"Thank—"

"One hopes to gain a little further insight into the top strata of this sector of our so-called civilisation."

"Thank you very much, Dr. Varga," said the young man, firmly but not loudly: he had no need to speak loudly because he now held the hand-microphone a few inches from his mouth.

Varga gave a brief nod, then showed his excellent teeth when he saw all attention being transferred to the arrival of (as it soon proved) Benedict Royal. Varga made his way through a lofty first-floor chamber that resembled the wartime operations room it had once in fact been. Maps, photographs, reports of all descriptions covered the long tables; to one side was a miniature radio, telephony and telegraphy station; of the dozens of thoroughly assorted police personnel, not one seemed idle.

At the far end were double doors leading into the conference-room, situated here so that the Special Investigatory Committee should maintain the closest touch with the police network. By the time Varga had taken his seat, and introductions been completed, the Committee was ready to begin its business. Charles Paynter rose to open the meeting in person at 0905. Forty minutes later he left for a meeting at 10 Downing Street, vacating the chair in favour of his Under-Secretary of State. On Lambert-Syme's right sat, in order, MacBean, Costello, Henderson, Young and (to Young's evident discomfort) Varga. Opposite them were ex-Detective Chief Super-intendent Barry, Commissioner Follett, Detective-Inspector Kemp and Benedict Royal. Most of the day's business passed in turning steadily through what was by now an immense pile of detail concerning the three murders.

The third murder had taken place some thirty-six hours previously. The victim, Janice Collins, aged 22, had been found lying stabbed to death near one of the roadways in Hyde Park. The multiplicity, nature and position of her wounds tallied with the facts of the first two cases. A fragment of newspaper pinned to her clothing contained the letter T and part of an H. As yet, nobody had reported seeing or hearing anything that might concern the crime, but police inquiries were continuing. Thanks to the drafting-in of hundreds of C.I.D. men from Forces outside London, more members of the public had already been interviewed, more state-ments already taken, than in any comparable period of investigation. Press and broadcasting coverage had been on a similar scale.

When all the material had been presented, Lambert-Syme called upon Barry to open the discussion. Barry, a

bald, fat, sleepy-looking figure in repose, was brisk
enough as soon as he started to speak.

> EXTRACTS FROM THE PROCEEDINGS OF THE SPE-
> CIAL INVESTIGATORY COMMITTEE, Day 1.
> Present: Barry, Costello, Follett, Hender-
> son, Kemp, Lambert-Syme, MacBean,
> Royal, Varga, Young.
> *Barry:* Let's begin as far back as we can. Three
> murders with the same weapon and by the
> same hand, judging from the angle and
> position and so on. Are you satisfied with
> that, Dr. Henderson?
> *Henderson:* From what you've shown me it's
> extremely likely. I'll accept it for the mo-
> ment.
> *Barry:* Thank you. Now as to the victims. No
> links between them established and none
> likely to be either. Contrasting types phys-
> ically and in other ways. Ainsworth was
> passable as regards looks, had one boy-
> friend and nobody much else. Buck was
> pretty and slept around. Collins was a
> virgin and no wonder, but she was good
> fun and had plenty of friends. Same sort of
> thing all the way through: nothing more in
> common than sex and age-group. That's
> quite a lot, though. Which takes us on to
> motive. If it's rational it's one I've never
> come across, unless it's cutting a dash in a
> big way, and that's not very rational either.

So I'm looking your way, Dr. Young, and
remember you can get as elementary as
you like without bothering me at all.

Young: Well, one type of violent psychopath
seems to be charged by a hatred of
women—Jack the Ripper and so on. But
there you tend to get excessive violence,
like the Ripper very much, and that's not
the case here—right, George?

Henderson: I'd agree, yes. With a blade like that
anybody who wasn't a doctor would need
to spread the wounds. In Collins's case,
you remember, only one of the four really
got home.

Young: Then there's the straightforward sadistic
sexual killing. Well, I suppose it isn't all
that straightforward. What I mean is, the
act of killing in itself is enough to . . .
satisfy the chap's urge, so there's no inter-
course or attempt at it. Then there are the
people who are really mad . . .

Lambert-Syme: Unlike the models of sanity
you've been telling us about.

Young: Sorry, I was thinking of the chap who
decides the world is such a wicked and
miserable place that he starts what he'd say
was giving other chaps a merciful release.
The trouble with—

Varga: [Inaudible]

Lambert-Syme: I'm sorry, Dr. Varga?

Varga: Just the obvious point that all what we

call violent crime is in essence this. A
protest against the evils of our society.

Barry: That's not quite the same thing, is it, Dr.
Varga? With respect, and even if it was, it
would sort of cancel out on both sides of
the equation and leave us back where we
were. Go on, please, Dr. Young.

Young: I was going to say, the kind of murder I
had in mind is usually a family affair. The
fellow knocks off his wife and kids, plus
any uncles and aunts who may be round
the place, and then himself, typically.

Costello: So the variety that interests you, Quintin, is variety number two, what you
called the straightforward sadistic killer.

Young: It's pretty rare, and they often don't
stick to women. As I said, it's taking life
they like. But yes, I favour number two at
this stage. As among psychopaths, that is.

Costello: I suppose we can rule out these people
who've written and telephoned in? The
Dark December lot and the—what were
they?—the British Liberation Army.

MacBean: We can rule out nobody, my dear Sir
Neil. Nobody, seeing that the laws of this
realm stand as they do.

Follett: [Erased from record]

Barry: Well, as regards that, I rather think we
can, sir, for the moment anyway. Special
Branch aren't exactly sitting on their bot-
toms, but they say it would be unique in a

big way, and my experience says the same.
Girls, not politicians or the law or security. And the method, it's so dangerous. A
bomb, gelignite, you're out of the way
when it happens. No, somebody's trying
to cash in is my guess. We won't forget it,
but I'll start taking them seriously when
they can show a connection, like telling us
something only the killer could know.
What do you think, Inspector Kemp?

Kemp: Oh. Oh, yes, Chief Superintendent, I
agree. Mind you, I haven't had much to do
with that side of life down where I am.
Where I usually am.

Barry: Let's move on, shall we, gentlemen?
This lull. Nothing last night. Not the end
of it: he couldn't find anyone safe or he
was otherwise engaged. It can't be the end,
if only because of these . . . perishing
letters. SOUTH. South what? Anybody . . . ?

Costello: South Yemen . . . Liberation Front?

Barry: I hope not, sir. That would mean, oh,
another twenty before he's done. I'm
afraid it looks like waiting and seeing
there. Now the girls' surnames, the A-B-C
question. To show they're linked? But any
fool can see that without. Mind you, it
could be chance.

Kemp: The chance of it being chance is of the
order of one in three thousand, I'm told,
sir.

Barry: That's not specially long odds in this kind of work. X-Y-Z would be a different matter. Well, a bit different.

Royal: Can I say something?

Lambert-Syme: Of course, Mr. Royal, please.

Royal: They're calling them the ABC Murders in the papers and places. That's what a book by Agatha Christie's called. I must have seen it on a news-stand somewhere.

Follett: It's been checked. No lead.

Royal: Are you sure, Commissioner? Just the title. And it's a book, isn't it? A story. Something someone made up. What I mean, what's been happening isn't . . . well, it isn't like it is. Is it, Chief Superintendent?

Barry: If you mean what I think you mean, no, it isn't.

Royal: Right, it's like a thriller. Whoever it is is doing a thriller. So I'd like to make a suggestion. I don't know much about them, but I do know, at least I know of, somebody who knows a lot. Somebody Dane. Christopher Dane?

Henderson: The James Fenton chap?

Royal: Right, James Fenton, Mr. Chairman, I move that Chistopher Dane be adopted on to this committee. It's not that I don't think the police are up to their job, Commissioner, but the Chief Superintendent agrees with me, this isn't like it is.

[The motion was eventually carried *nem. con.*,
Follett, MacBean, and Varga abstaining.]

The meeting broke up shortly before seven o'clock.
Lambert-Syme and MacBean left for the House of
Commons, where a division was thought to be imminent;
Kemp said he must be getting back to his local crime
squad; in passing, Royal mentioned a television appearance; Varga, whose contribution to the day's work had
been a total of four closely similar references to our
society and its less than robust state of health, swept out
in silence; Follett, Young and Henderson decided to go
out together for dinner; pressed to join them, Barry
resisted, explaining that he must look over the regional
reports again to fix them in his mind, and that he would
not go short of sustenance, what with sandwiches from
the canteen and Scotch from the drinks-tray in the
conference-room itself.

Another amenity of that room was a large television
set. When the time came, Barry switched it on and
watched the News, partly by way of relief from his
labours, partly to see how far and in what direction the
facts about the murders and the investigation of them
would be distorted. Not far, he had to admit, and in the
comparatively harmless direction of suggesting that such
brains as those concerned must soon solve the problem
by the pure light of reason. Better than the truth,
anyway, reflected Barry: to wit, that on summons from
politicians much more interested in public opinion than
in public safety, a roomful of well-meaning but ineffec-
tive masterminds, undisguised crackpots, mystified and

frightened coppers, plus one unknown quantity (Royal) had spent a long day getting nowhere slowly. The thought of Royal had barely passed from Barry's mind when that very name was spoken by the newsreader and Royal himself appeared on the screen. Not a bad-looking lad, Barry had to concede, and his shortish hair, clean-shaven face and quiet style of dress made him hard to associate with the world in which he had earned his money and fame. When he spoke, his voice and manner were likewise restrained, though earnest. He said into the camera:

"As you heard, there's a killer on the loose. The police are doing all they can, but they can't protect everyone in the Greater London area. So you've got to protect yourselves. After dark, try not to go anywhere alone. If you can't avoid doing this, don't have anything to do with anyone you don't know. Anyone at all. Keep away from open spaces—parks, commons, bits of waste ground. If you see anything. . . ."

A buzzer and a winking red light showed that the conference-room loudspeaker had been brought into circuit with one of the police channels in the next room. Barry flipped a switch and listened for about a quarter of a minute, making a note or two on a pad. He switched off and was hurrying for the door when one of the outside-line telephones rang. After an instant's violent hesitation he answered it.

"Barry here. . . . Yes, Peter . . . Yes, indeed there is. Another one. But still alive."

CHAPTER THREE

E x-Detective Chief Superintendent Barry ran into the main entrance-hall of the hospital and was immediately taken to the lifts by the uniformed constable who had awaited him. They were still on the ground floor when Special Commissioner Peter Follett joined them. On the way up Barry asked:

"Are we in time?"

"A quarter of an hour ago you were, sir; I don't know about now."

"Has she said anything?"

"I'm afraid I don't know that either, sir. . . . This way, please."

Barry and Follett hurried into a room where half a dozen figures were clustered at a bedside. All of them made some sort of turning-away movement at the pair's arrival, but not, Barry saw within a second, in response to it. He gave a small sigh.

"Gone, has she?"

A doctor spoke. "Not yet, no. But for your purposes she had."

"Did you get anything at all?"

"Oh yes, sir, quite a lot." This was the local police superintendent. "It's all here, on paper and on tape."

"Let's hear that tape. Leave your shorthand man with her. I'm sorry, doctor, I'm not questioning your competence, but–"

"Of course."

Three minutes later, in the doctor's clean, tidy and uncomfortable office, Barry was saying,

"Identification?"

"Name of Sandra Phillips, sir," said a plain-clothes man. "Lives nearby. There's a husband, but we haven't found him yet."

Follett had glanced abruptly at Barry. "What was that about odds of three thousand to one against the A-B-C sequence being chance?"

"I said that was pretty short odds, didn't I? Married, too."

"If you're interested in odds," said the doctor, "I'd have given something in that range against her having survived more than a minute or two after being attacked. Eleven wounds."

"God Almighty," said Barry. "Oh well. Age?"

"About thirty."

"Another break in the pattern," said Follett.

"Mm." Barry rubbed his eyes wearily. "We might as well have the tape."

Questioning of Sandra
Phillips: [Pauses and repetition of questions not
  indicated.]
Did you see the person who attacked you?
Yes.
Was it a man?
Yes.
Can you describe him?
He was rather old. About forty. Grey hair. Not
  very tall. Rather fat.
What was he wearing?
An old overcoat. Brown. And a hat. An old
  hat.
Did he say anything?
Yes. He wanted me to help him. To find a
  house.
What house?
[No answer]
What was his voice like?
Nothing special. Rather deep.
What sort of accent?
Like the BBC. There was another man as well.
*What? What was he like? Did you get a good look at
  him?*
Very tall. Rather thin. He had an Irish accent.
What did he say?
We've come to get you, Sandra.
Anything else?
He's ill. He must be ill.
Who? What did he mean?
[Inaudible]

Can you tell us anything more about this other man?
[No answer]

The plain-clothes man switched off the recorder. After
a pause, during which cups of what was called coffee
arrived and were distributed, Barry said,
"Sandra . . . Right, what else have you got? Just
essentials for now. Doctor?"
"I've read the papers and I've heard things. The
wounds are consistent with that, although of course one
can't be really sure at this stage. In the same sort of way,
no obvious sign of sexual . . . activity."
"Thank you." Barry turned wordlessly to the local
police chief.
"Nothing so far where the girl was found. Except on
her clothing—letters clipped from a newspaper, the
righthand half of an H, it looks like, and an E. No sign
at the moment that she fought her attacker."
"I see," said Barry. "Come in," he added in response to
a knock on the door.
"She's dead, sir."

EXTRACTS FROM THE PROCEEDINGS OF THE SPE-
CIAL INVESTIGATORY COMMITTEE, Day 2.
Present: Lambert-Syme (in the chair),
Barry, Costello, Dane, Follett, Hender-
son, Kemp, MacBean, Royal, Varga,
Young.
Barry: One of them was genuine, in the sense
that he knew how much this British Lib-
eration Army lot had asked for the first

time. "We want double now—two hundred thousand." But the fact he had an
Irish accent means nothing at all. There's
plenty of people about ready to grab a fiver
for making a 'phone call without the slightest risk, and some of 'em are going to be
Irishmen. Only thing it shows, they read
the papers. There's still nothing whatso-
ever to connect them with the murders.
I'm not saying it couldn't be them, just
there's no reason to think it is and a lot of
reason to think it isn't.

Costello: As regards this last atrocity—are we
sure this isn't a crime of imitation? The
docks at Rotherhithe are a long way from
Hyde Park, and I don't just mean geo-
graphically. And her attackers seeming to
know her. . . .

Barry: I'd say her mind was wandering at that
point. No sense in it any other way.
Anyhow, the forensic reporter's conclu-
sive: this is more of the same.

Costello: So we're left with our psychopath, are
we? Or now it seems a pair of psychopaths. Wouldn't you say that that was
rather unlikely?

Henderson: Folie à deux?

Royal: That's a load of rubbish, isn't it?

Varga: Folie à tout le monde.

Lambert-Syme: No doubt. Your department,
Quintin.

Young: Yes, the idea that two people who aren't psychopathic individually behave psychopathically in concert, well, it doesn't seem to stand up. The view is that the senior partner is a genuine psychopath with some strong emotional hold over the junior partner. Who stops behaving psychopathically when separated from the senior partner. See Brady and Hindley. As for a couple of genuine psychopaths working together, it's unlikely. Individualistic lot, psychopaths.

Barry: So it's more likely to be one madman plus a chap who behaves like a madman than two madmen. I see.

Young: Well, not mad, but . . . Never mind.

Lambert-Syme: Any comments, Mr. Dane? Mr. Dane.

Dane: What? No. Sorry.

Henderson: Are you unwell, Mr. Dane?

Dane: No. No, I'm all right. Thank you.

"Are you really all right, Mr. Dane?" asked Henderson when the meeting adjourned for lunch.

"Yes, of course." Dane lowered his voice abruptly. "No. I'm not. I'm not ill, not physically, but I'm not all right."

"What's the trouble?"

"Answer me one question and I'll consider telling you. I don't care if you think I'm mad."

"I dare say you don't, but you ought to care if Dr.

Young thinks you're mad, so I suggest you put your question to him as well."

"If you like."

"Quintin . . . Mr. Dane has a question which may make you think he's mad."

"Please don't be flippant, Dr. Henderson: this is very serious. Or it may be; I'd like your advice on that. Now. Have you solid alibis for these murders, any or all of them?"

The look on Henderson's face went a long way towards justifying Dane's forebodings but Young answered readily enough.

"Very solid for at least two of them. Dr. Henderson and I were in each other's company at the relevant time on the evening of the second murder and again last night, when Commissioner Follett was also present."

"Other witnesses on the evening of the second murder?"

"Oh yes. Servants at the Irving Club; fellow members."

"Very satisfactory. Now I can tell you why I'm not all right, or how, anyway. Not here, though. Is there a pub handy?"

"Well, we had a sort of half-arrangement with Follett. We could–"

"Put him off."

"But as I said, he was—"

"Please, Dr. Young."

"What I'm going to tell you," said Dane, as the three sat in a comparatively quiet corner of the pub that had proved to be handy, "will probably sound a shade madder than my original question, but I still don't mind."

"Let's dispose of that right away." Young sipped at his pint of bitter. "I say, aren't these brewers lucky to be so successful? You're not mad. Normally I'd need to know you better than I do to be so positive, but I've read a couple of your books, and that's enough."

"You mean a book can tell you whether its author's mad or not?"

"Oh yes. Christopher Dane understands human motives—I'm not talking about motives for murder and so on, just motives, motives for ordinary behavior. To the mad, other people are . . . a closed book. You might be a psychopath, of course, but I see no signs of it."

"You were making that distinction at the meeting. I couldn't see what the hell you were talking about."

"The psychopath understands other people when he bothers to; he just doesn't care about the consequences of his actions. Takes no thought for the morrow."

"Wasn't that chap Neville Heath, the one who cut those girls up, wasn't he a psychopath?"

"Oh, classic case."

"He took no thought for the morrow in a big way."

"And in smaller ways from puberty onwards. Take the question of his—"

"Look, don't let's take any bloody Heath questions at all," interrupted Henderson. "We came here to listen to this fellow's story, not Heath's."

"Sorry."

"You needn't apologise to me, Dr. Young. It's no waste of my time to be told on good authority that I'm not mad and to be enabled to deduce that I'm not a psychopath. Especially after. . . . Anyway, there are two bits to this. I'm telling you the first because you may think that, not apparently the balance of my mind, thank God, but my judgment may be impaired, which is important with the second bit.

"First bit. I'm working on a new book at the moment. At least I was. The plot's about a psychopathic killer who goes round stabbing girls."

"Quite a coincidence," said Young brightly. "Is that all of the first bit?"

"Isn't it enough? Well, no, it's not all. I kept getting the feeling I was responsible in some way."

"You mean a burglar broke into your house to pinch the silver, started reading your manuscript out of curiosity, and ended up saying to himself, 'Hey, why am I wasting my time pinching silver when I could be out stabbing girls?' Or perhaps your wife or your charwoman. . . ."

"I know it was ridiculous of me."

"It doesn't sound all that ridiculous to me," said Henderson, "but then I'm not a student of the mind."

"Thank you. Ridiculous or not, I couldn't work and I couldn't sleep; all I could do was follow the case in the papers and on radio and television. Allow for that when I tell you the second bit. Here it is. One of the murderers is a member of this committee. Perhaps both."

"You must be . . ." began Henderson.

"Mad. Ha ha. Or joking. Not joking. That chap Royal, bright lad by the way, he got it right when he said—I've read the transcripts of your first session—

when he said whoever it was was doing a thriller. In a thriller, the guilty party would have to be on the committee, wouldn't he? In fact, by rights it ought to be Royal himself, because he suggested co-opting me."

"Let's get this straight." Young drained his tankard and made a face. "Now I'm not joking either. The criminal started his activities equipped with the foreknowledge that a committee of exactly this sort would be set up and that he'd be able to get himself appointed to it. Is that what you're saying?"

"Of course not. All I'm saying is that when the committee was set up our man or men had a chance of joining in, and grabbed the chance, firstly as a means of keeping up with how close the police might be getting, and secondly because it made the whole thing into a rather better class of thriller."

"Oh, that's all you're saying? Well, you'd know, of course, but I'd have thought it would have the opposite effect. The whole structure would be founded not on a grand design but on a titanic piece of luck. It was overwhelmingly unlikely that anything but a special squad of coppers would have been formed."

"Was it?" Dane sounded a little pugnacious. "To deal with what's becoming a national emergency? A criminal lawyer is just the sort of man they'd pick, for one. And the lawyer they did pick turns out to be an Irishman. A tall Irishman."

Henderson said sharply, "That's nonsense. Just to begin with, Neil's been living in this country for about forty years. Indistinguishable from an Englishman."

"Have you ever met a Welshman or a Yorkshireman

who couldn't do a bit of local dialect however posh or English or Southern he talked normally?"

"If that's enough for you to start a theory on you're pretty easily satisfied."

"Oh, I'm not in sight of a theory yet. Just following up my original hunch. No, I don't care for the word, either. But it can't be denied that there's such a thing. So strong in this case that I had to insist on eliminating the two of you before I started. Having hunches is what I'm here for."

"All right, you're excused," said Henderson. "I think that must be our food. It's okay; I'll get it."

While Henderson was pushing his way through to the bar, Dane turned to Young and, with a return to his earlier look of unease, said:

"I'm going to sound ridiculous again, but to hell with it. Could I have done those murders, or helped to do them, and then forgotten about it?"

"No." Young was emphatic. "Anyway, you're bound to have alibis for a couple of them surely."

"I haven't got alibis for any of them. I'm temporarily living away from home to get my book done in peace. It's my usual arrangement."

"Except that this time you're not getting your book done."

"I may be able to now you've put my mind at rest."

"Has the plot got a committee of inquiry in it?"

"No. The whole thing's solved by my freelance chap."

"I see."

The food arrived. Dane said:

"There is one fact I've been keeping up my sleeve. Not

a very big one, I'm afraid, but anyway. As I said, I've
been following all the public reports. None of them has
mentioned the number of wounds inflicted in any of the
cases. "Multiple wound," "repeatedly stabbed" and so
on. Somebody's rule about not causing unnecessary
distress—I don't know. In fact, they weren't all that
multiple until the last one. For instance, Collins was
stabbed four times. Only one of the four—what was it,
Dr. Henderson?—"really got home." Who knows that,
apart from the police and medical chaps immediately
concerned with the case? The members of the Committee. So it's interesting that Phillips was stabbed eleven
times. He, or they, meant to make sure; the fact that the
opposite happened doesn't matter. Suggestive, wouldn't
you say?"

"These sausages are rather on the authentic side."
Young took a fragment from his mouth. "Statutory
proportion of gristle and chunks of bone. Well yes, Mr.
Dane, very dimly and uncertainly suggestive. Have you
any more suggestiveness?"

"Not yet. The fact that the next one will be done with
a different weapon doesn't mean anything, because
everybody knows now that Phillips survived for that
crucial time. But it does show the reason for the letters,
the SOUTH business." When neither of the other two
spoke or even looked up, Dane hurried on, "You don't
need them to establish a link if other things are doing that
too—Superintendent Barry's point. But you do need
them if you change the other things: the method, for
instance."

Young lit a cigarette. "Does your hunch extend to the question why a link should be desirable?"

"No. Classically—I mean in detective stories the link is a misdirection, with the killer disguising the one murder he really wants to commit as nothing more than an item in a programme of mass murders. Phillips is the least unlikely candidate, but she didn't move in circles where you knock off three girls on the other side of London so as to get away with knocking her off. Either there's no central murder or we haven't got to it yet. I'm in the dark about motives, you see."

"I'm not surprised," said Henderson.

"Oh, I don't mean I can't think of any. MacBean wants to shock the nation into restoring capital punishment. Royal's record sales are dropping, so he's going to make sure of being famous for something else. Varga hates women—remember that wife of his who committed suicide?—and is also a lunatic. Costello, a great prosecuting lawyer, so could be a sadist."

For a moment, unnoticed by Dane or Henderson, Young's face showed disquiet, even alarm. Then he said lightly, "And so on and so on."

"Okay. Well, you can see why I didn't want the Commissioner to hear any of this. Thank you for not actually bursting out laughing yourselves. Now: will you send me home, Dr. Henderson? As suffering from 'flu, say. I seem to have looked indisposed enough this morning. There's a spot of unofficial nosing-about I want to do while you're all confabulating up there. Thanks again. I'll be seeing you."

When Dane had gone, Young and Henderson ordered

large Scotches. The pub had begun to empty and they drank standing at the bar.

"Well, he may not be mad," said Henderson. "I'll take your word for that."

"But being a bloody fool is something else again."

"That's a bit hard. As he said, his job is to make guesses along whodunit lines. And nobody else has any ideas at all."

"Ideas are two a penny."

"Here's one that's maybe worth a little more. I took his point that Royal should be the guilty party because of co-opting him; Dane, that is. It would be grander still if Dane set the whole thing up himself as a practical exercise in his art, with him playing both criminal and detective. What fun if he happened to have no alibis for the vital times."

Young sipped his whisky with a thoughtful air.

"I do wish you'd go up to bed, dear," said Mrs. Addams to her husband. "What's the use of staying home if you don't go up to bed?"

"I'm all right, dear. I'm quite happy in front of the fire."

"I wish you'd stay there at least, instead of sitting out in that draughty old shed till all hours of the night. It's what's given you this chill."

"It isn't a chill, dear, no more than a slight cold on the chest. I'm really pampering myself staying home at all. And I'll have you know that shed, as you see fit to call it, isn't draughty."

"All right, dear. I'm sorry. Now you sit there nice and comfortable while I go out and get you the paper."

"Thank you, dear."

"It beats me why you need it, what with all the news on the wireless and the television, but I know you've got your work to do."

When he was sure his wife had left the house, Henry Addams made his way to the kitchen, pausing once for a hearty bout of coughing: he was in some real discomfort. He opened a drawer by the sink, revealing a number of knives, one of which he picked out and examined closely. As he tested its point against his thumb, his breathing quickened and he started to cough again.

"Can I help you, sir?" asked the man in hall-porter's uniform, laying down his newspaper.

"I was looking for Mr. MacBean."

"Out, sir. Never in before nine and often not then when they're sitting late."

"Perhaps I could have a word with his secretary."

"You could not, sir. He don't have a secretary, not full-time. Some days he has a girl in."

"Lives alone, does he?"

"Yeah. What's it to you, anyway?"

"Sorry, I should have said. *Evening Chronicle.*" A pound note was put down and picked up. "Perhaps you can help me."

"I'll try, sir."

"We're doing a feature on how famous people get about London with all the traffic, and considering how much Mr. MacBean must move around, we thought—"

"You're right there, sir. Always on the go, old Fergie.
Well, he don't run a car. Very sensible, too, these days.
Uses a hire firm, he does."

"Thanks very much."

The porter looked closely at his questioner. "I'd have
thought they'd have sent a boy to find out that."

"I bet you would, mate, but you don't know our
Features Editor. It's off your backside and on the spot
when you're doing a job for him. I'll be lucky if I'm
through before eight tonight. You must work a long day,
too, but at least you're indoors."

"Oh, I'm available at any time, except when I'm not.
You'd be amazed how many hours I spend not being
available," said the man, as if advertising some rare
amenity. "Of course, later on you have to have a key. I
wouldn't leave the place wide open."

"Sure. Thanks again."

Outside the block of flats, Christopher Dane walked
slowly and without much air of purpose to the nearest
corner. Here he paused, looked about, and saw something. It was only an Underground station sign, but its
effect on him was marked. He strode off and was soon
running for a taxi. Twenty minutes later he rang the door
bell of a house in Eaton Square. After a long pause, a
flabby-faced woman opened the door and leaned against
the jamb.

"Yes?"

"Lady Costello?"

"Yes."

"I'm from Circumspect Insurance. It's about your

husband's car. Seems somebody ran into it where it was parked. Where would that be?"

"Sorry, where would what be?"

"Where does your husband normally park his car?"

"Somewhere round. Round here. Has he had an accident or something?"

"No, he's all right. Did he spend yesterday evening at home?"

"Yes. Well, some of it. He must have done. Sorry, I think I must have been a bit sloshed. He was here this morning."

"Thank you, I've got that," said Dane. Peering at a blank page of his notebook, he added, "And you have two servants living in, is that correct?"

"No, it isn't correct. They go away . . . later on. Listen, would you like a drink? No, you're on duty."

"I'm afraid so, madam, but thank you very kindly for the offer. Now I must be on my way."

"Sorry if I . . ."

"Perfectly all right, madam. Good afternoon."

Dane walked away, chuckling slightly and shaking his head.

"We shouldn't despise those early figures who diagnosed the sickness of our society," said Marcus Varga earnestly. "When there are no doctors, you must give attention to the wise woman of the village; where there are no drugs, you must know of the folk remedies. But these primitive days are finished. They were guessing; we know."

"I've always thought we've got a sick society," said his companion. "All this affluence. And the environment.

"These are the symptoms of something deeper. And here we must drop the analogy with medical science—a foolish and imprecise term. Except in the crudest manner, medicine cannot predict. If you smoke many cigarettes, you may some time later develop lung cancer, emphysema and these things. But not always. They haven't established a cause-and-effect situation already, and they never will.

"They ought to legalise hash. It's repression and arbitrary not to.

"But so-called civilisation is not like the human body. Here, if we know the technique, we can predict. We . . . but this is very rude of me. You must allow me to buy a drink. But first I must introduce myself. I am Michael Vernon."

"Linda Harris."

"And what can I get you, Linda?"

"I'd like a rum and Coke, please."

Varga, in expensive black corduroy, crossed the fashionably semi-dark bar to the counter. While he waited for service he looked unobtrusively about him. No one, it seemed, was paying him the slightest attention. He noted the time: nine twenty. Soon his turn came for ordering and he carried the drinks over to the curtained alcove where he had got into conversation with Linda Harris ten minutes earlier.

"I don't know how you can do with gin and tonic in this weather."

"Oh, I'm a very warm person, Linda." Varga did not offer the information that his glass contained nothing but tonic water and ice.

"You're not from here, are you?"

"No, I'm American. And that means, of course, that I do have a close knowledge of society at its most rotten."

"All the ghettos and Watergate."

They went on like that for another quarter of an hour or so. Then Varga said, "Shall we continue this marvelous discussion where it's quieter and more comfortable? My little house is only a few minutes away."

"Well . . . all right."

They left the bar. Holding the girl gently by the elbow, Varga steered her along the pavement. Most of the buildings here were shops, now closed, and there were not many people about.

"I think it isn't quite so cold," he said.

"Have you got a car?"

"Oh, we can walk there."

They reached the end of the row of shops and the edge of an expanse of grassland. A line of street-lamps marked its further boundary, but the intervening area, a few hundred yards across, was dark.

"You can almost see it from here," said Varga. "Just where the lights go level, about the hill."

"I'm not going across there."

"It's not wet, and we come soon to a path."

"I don't care, I'm not going. The police have warned people not to go with anyone they don't know, and I don't know you."

"So you do as the pigs tell you, eh?"

"This time I do. I'm sorry: you seem all right, but I can't be sure, and that's that."

"So you think I'd have talked to you in there with all those people around if I was going to . . . ?"

"I don't think anything."

"We'll walk round the long way by the streets if you like," said Varga.

But he said it to a retreating back. He bared his teeth and breathed hard through them, then relaxed totally, looked at his watch again, and hurried off the way he had come.

Benedict Royal slid into the passenger seat of the Oldsmobile and clicked the door to. "Right, Marty. Home. Quick as you like."

Mannheim set the car going and some minutes passed in silence. Royal seemed to doze. Then Mannheim said, "How'd it go?"

"Like a dream."

"You'll get caught sooner or later. Bound to."

"Relax, old fellow. Only three more of these. And what do you care if I do get caught? You haven't done anything."

"I'm doing this, that's enough. If you go down you'll take me with you, you know that. I don't know why I let myself get mixed up in it."

"Yes, it is a mystery. A little thing like the threat of being sacked if you didn't, plus enough bad talk to see to it you never got to be anybody else's manager, that's not enough to shake our Marty. Forget it. How many coming in?"

"Oh, not a lot. Twenty?"

"Good sluts?"

"You know me. Hand-picked."

"Good. I'm on the look-out tonight."

"What do you mean?"

"A successor to Miss Priest."

"I get it, Benedict, but little Karen isn't going to take kindly to being given the brush."

"Unkindly's fine with me. You know the old routine. A cheque starring the figure zero in one hand and a fist in the other."

"Karen just might be the sort to pick the fist."

"I said unkindly was fine with me."

"Then she goes and shows her face to the fuzz."

"No sweat. The fuzz and me were at school together and you were with me when it didn't happen."

"Be a good boy and give the cheque the hard sell."

"Yes, Marty. I'll do as you say, Marty."

The car pulled off the roadway into a semicircular gravel drive and stopped at a stone portico. A short flight of steps led up to the front door of the house. On either side of these steps there was an area separated from the drive by a low wall.

About to open his car door, Royal said, "What time did you tell them to come?"

"Midnight."

"Someone's jumped the gun. I say, Carruthers, what frightfully bad form."

At the far end of the drive another car was to be seen, not very clearly seen in the poor light. Royal and Mannheim got out of the Oldsmobile and began to move towards the flight of steps. They still had some yards to go when a strange and terrible clamour started up from

the distant car; to anyone unfamiliar with it, it might
have sounded like a battery of pneumatic drills. The air
round the two in front of the house was filled with
whipping noises, pieces of gravel and chips of stone. A
ground-floor window shattered in an instant.

"Over the wall, Marty," shouted Royal.

Each made for the area nearest to him, and each
arrived there. The din ceased abruptly. There were cries
within the house and a first-floor window was thrown
up. Then a voice spoke, an unnaturally loud voice,
agreed later by those who had heard it to be amplified by
some sort of megaphone. It said:

"With the compliments of the British Liberation
Army!"

The accent was Irish.

"Did you hit him, do you think, Sean?"

"Don't talk. Drive."

Ronnie Grainger drove very fast indeed for the minute
or so required to bring the car (stolen earlier that evening)
into traffic; then it slowed to a normal pace, as prearranged.

"Well, come on, did you hit him?"

"I don't know. In a way I hope not."

"Why?"

"Well, in the first place it was agreed I shouldn't, and
you know I'm a great one for keeping to agreements
whenever possible. And in the second place, whatever
you may think, I'm opposed to the unnecessary taking of
human life."

"Call that a human life?"

Sean looked at Grainger for a moment. "Sure: who am I to discriminate? It's hard not to hit someone when your object is to show you're really trying to. Anyway, we've attained that object all right."

CHAPTER FOUR

EXTRACT FROM THE PROCEEDINGS OF THE SPE-
CIAL INVESTIGATORY COMMITTEE, DAY 3.
Present: Lambert-Syme (in the chair),
Barry, Costello, Dane, Follett, Hender-
son, Kemp, MacBean, Royal, Varga,
Young.

Royal: Sorry I'm late, everybody. Quite a lot of
people seemed to have nothing better to do
than hang around my house. The police
couldn't hold 'em. Tried all they could of
course.

Lambert-Syme: I'm sure everybody understands,
Mr. Royal. It's most creditable on your
part to have ventured out after your dis-
tressing ordeal.

Royal: Oh, I was only shaken up—soon passed.

It's poor old Marty I'm sorry for. Mr.
Mannheim, I mean. But what a terrific
spirit he's got.

Henderson: How is he?

Royal: Well, he was out for nearly half an hour
after that bash on the head he gave himself, and he looks pretty rough to me, but
he's talking about getting up already. Anyway, thank God he wasn't hit.

[General murmurs of agreement, commiser-
ation, etc.]

Dane: May I ask Mr. Royal something? Did you
have the impression that both Mr. Mannheim and you were being shot at, or was it
only yourself?

Royal: Well, we were so close together you
couldn't tell.

Dane: You were standing absolutely side by
side?

Royal: Not standing—walking slowly, strolling.
Anyway, what of it?

Lambert-Syme: Yes, could we get on, gentlemen? You've got the preliminary reports in
front of you . . . Pauline Hodges . . .
26 years old . . . kitchen knife . . . A
and part of an S . . . mm . . . large
naevus on right cheek. Port-wine mark
that is, isn't it? Poor little creature, she
can't have had much of what makes life
worth living. Would you take it from
there, Bill?

Barry: The letters match with the others. S O
U T H E A S is what we've got now, so it
looks like we get the rest of the S and a T
next time. South-east or south-eastern
what? Anybody got any ideas? Nor me.
London postal district? Suppose it is—
where could that put us? He means he
lives in SE5, say. Oh really? Or he's been
to south-east Asia for his holidays. Interesting, eh? Nothing's emerged from any of
the investigations. Oh, a bloody mountain's *emerged*, but none of it hangs
together. No pattern.

Varga: Surely there are two things that now
hang together: these murders and the so-
called British Liberation Army. We should
make a start to pay them this money.

MacBean: We cannot afford to submit to blackmail, Dr. Varga. If you pay the black-
mailer, he comes back for more. His appe-
tite grows with what it feeds on.

Varga: But lives are in danger, including our
own lives. It's only a miracle that Mr.
Royal escaped. The next one of us may not
be so fortunate.

Follett: Dr. Varga, there's nothing whatever to
suggest that any further attempts will be
made on members of this Committee, because there's nothing to suggest that Mr.
Royal was fired on in his capacity as a
member, so to speak. A public figure—

Varga: I'm not going to die for your theories, Commissioner, I demand a police guard.

Follett: Look, if you knew how many . . . Tell him, Bill.

Barry: Effective round-the-clock protection for the lot of us would take over a hundred men, and at the moment I haven't got one to spare.

MacBean: Our safety lies with the safety of all, in catching these malefactors; I would not allow a single officer of the law to be deviated from that duty in order to look after me.

Royal: Right.

Lambert-Syme: Is everybody satisfied? You can always resign if you feel nervous, Dr. Varga.

Varga: It's my role to remain.

Lambert-Syme: As you wish. Bill, from what you were saying to me just now you still don't buy the idea of a connection between this confounded British Liberation Army and the killings. Would you expound?

Barry: The only connection is an Irish accent, and there are plenty of them in London. They know it's all they've got. Why do they shout at Mr. Royal and take a risk doing it? Because you can't write a note in an Irish accent. And as I've said all along, why not use bombs from the start?

Royal: Not atrocious enough. People are used to

bombs these days. These stabbings and
things get on everybody's nerves.

Barry: Fair point, Mr. Royal, but, as before, I'll
consider believing in a link when I see
one—in other words a communication
from these blokes that has something in it
that only the killer could know. Oh, we're
combing the Irishmen, but I've no great
hopes there. One thing is, all this TV
coverage on Ulster and so on means a
passable mimic could do a passable Irish
accent.

Royal: I'd swear it was genuine, what I heard.
Genuine Ulster, in fact.

Lambert-Syme: Isn't there anything positive we
can do, anything at all? The Press are
yelling their heads off and I can't say I
blame them. The Minister's position is
becoming—

Follett: The Minister can . . .

Costello: What about doubling the reward?

Follett: Or promising the killer immunity and a
first-class flight to South America if he
gives himself up.

Young: What's the position on discharged psychopathic patients, Bill?

Barry: Like the Irishmen, we're looking
through them.

Varga: They should be left alone. They are
victims of our diseased society.

MacBean: If our society is diseased, the respon-

> sibility lies very largely at the door of such
> as you, Dr. Varga.
> *Varga:* On the contrary, Mr. MacBean, of you
> and your kind . . .

After what seemed a very long time to most of those
present, the Committee broke up, pledging itself to
reconvene at 2:30. Lambert-Syme declared roundly that
one should not keep a lady waiting and strode out. The
others followed at a slower pace, Barry and Follett
evidently in the deepest gloom. Dane approached Young
and Henderson.

"I've found out one or two things. Care to hear them?"

Young glanced at his friend. "Well, after Varga and
MacBean I could do with a little light relief. But that
pub's a straightforward hell-hole."

"There's a sort of bistro round the corner that doesn't
look too bad," said Henderson.

They were soon installed in it, among climbing plants
and tanks of sluggish tropical fish. The waiter's apron
and fingernails were dirty. Young sent Henderson a glare
easily translatable into a trenchant criticism of the latter's
powers of perception. Over a glass of Valpolicella, Dane
outlined his discoveries of the previous afternoon. When
he had finished, Henderson said:

"So MacBean could have got in and out of his flat
without being seen, out and in, rather, or just in, and he
could have travelled to and from the scenes of the various
crimes by Tube. Have you checked that he really could
have done that?—I mean, that the places are within easy
distance of Tube stations?"

"Oh yes, and they all are except the last. A mile maximum for the first four. Hodges at the West India Docks would have been a bit more of a problem. A good two-mile slog to Wapping or Shadwell—they're roughly equidistant. Taxi in that area unlikely and he couldn't have relied on it. But far from impossible on foot. Interesting that it's only the last one that's difficult from the Underground point of view. As if—I'm guessing—as if he'd foreseen me deciding the Underground was the key and wanted to throw me off. As I say, though, still perfectly feasible. Especially with the killings apparently taking place well before midnight. Plenty of time before the trains stopped running."

"I'm not sure I know just where these damn places are," said Henderson after a pause. "Rotherhithe? West India Docks?"

"Just across the river from Bow. You know, Bow Bells and so on. A bike ride."

Young poured wine. "Three parks, or bits of open ground, then two sets of docks. Is that a pattern? And aren't docks rather well frequented, even after dark?"

"Not at the moment, I imagine, with a strike on. About as little frequented as parks are at that sort of time."

"Mm. He'd have to show his ticket and so on on the Tube."

"Very little risk of being recognised. His face isn't all that well known, and a simple false moustache and/or pair of heavy spectacles would fool any untrained observer. As regards alibis, that's where I'm hopelessly handicapped. I can't ask him and I can't ask the police to ask him; I'm not, er, foolish enough to think I can go to them at this stage. There is one rather nice thing though. I read in the paper he was speaking at a dinner on the night when there wasn't a murder. What do you call that? An inverted non-alibi?"

"Those scenes of the crimes. Have you tried linking them up on the map into any kind of shape?" asked Young.

Dane gave him a grateful look. "I like the way you're thinking. Yes, but there's nothing there yet. No straight lines, unless possibly numbers two, three and four were intended to be one and he slipped up. No right angles—again, numbers one, two and three nearly were, and I was expecting something round about Battersea Park for number four, but then he shoots clear across London. If there is any sort of picture, it won't emerge until as near the end of the series as possible, and judging by the letters we're still a long way from the end. I wish I had any idea of the point of them. I've tried rearranging—"

"Now Costello." Young was watching Dane closely. "You can't find out where he keeps his car and you think his wife's an alcoholic, so she couldn't give him an alibi. Is that the lot?"

"I'm afraid so. Sounds pathetic, doesn't it? There's a little on a couple of the others. Lambert-Syme must be out of it. Public alibis for Buck and Collins, and he lives—"

"So his confederate does Buck and Collins."

"Oh, there can't be a confederate," said Dane, sounding quite shocked. "It must be all one chap. So: Varga—

lives alone nowadays, and we agree on the hatred-of-women thing. Royal . . ."

"Royal's good," said Henderson, "because he set up that shooting incident himself to divert suspicion."

"You two are really beginning to appeal to me." Dane poured more wine. "A pity this Mannheim character will never be able to tell us anything about the circumstances of that. Your surprise is rather unflattering, Dr. Henderson. Even humble detective-story writers know that unconsciousness means concussion and concussion means amnesia."

"I wonder if Royal knows that."

"He couldn't count on there being a bang on the head, could he? Unless of course he delivered it himself."

"That would be nice."

"I like the attitude to spaghetti here," said Young, rolling some round on his fork. "They know it makes you fat and doesn't do you any good, so they cook it like this to see you don't eat much of it. Anything more on Royal?"

"No, except he didn't want police protection this morning, because police protection means in effect police surveillance."

"Varga wanted it, though."

"So he said. He can't be mad enough not to know he wasn't going to get it." While they waited, rather apprehensively, for coffee, Henderson asked Dane, "Do you take any stock in this British Liberation Army notion?"

"No. Barry's right on that. He's right on a lot of things."

"I thought the police were always wrong in your world."

"No, no, no." Dane sounded shocked again. "They're always right up to a point."

"Thank you for a most entertaining lunch," said Young to Dane a little later.

"Thank you for listening. Where's Henderson?"

"Gone to the gents, I imagine. Tell me, are you back at home now?"

"No, I'm still in my flat. I've got a lot of thinking to do."

"Is your flat like MacBean's? No effective supervision?"

"Well yes, it is. Why?"

"Just that, if you were in my shoes, you might find that . . . suggestive?"

The Committee had fully shaken off the rather bemused tranquillity that had reigned before the midday adjournment. In the outer room, Barry was talking fast into a telephone, Lambert-Syme waiting at another with an aspect of ungovernable impatience. Two men who might have been messengers were listening to a very shaken Follett. Costello and Royal stood at the central table and gazed at a sheet of paper on it. Young hurried up to them and looked over their shoulders. On the paper were the words.

OUR LAST MURDER VICTIM HAD
LARGE PORT-WINE MARK ON RIGHT
CHEEK. IF THIS DOESN'T CONVINCE

YOU THEN YOU ARE MAD. COLLECT
150 THOUSAND POUNDS IN OLD FIV-
ERS AND AWAIT INSTRUCTIONS FOR
PICKUP BY OUR MAN TONIGHT. BE
WARNED THAT IF HE IS ARRESTED
OR FOLLOWED WE WILL STRIKE
AGAIN. STAND BY FROM ELEVEN PM
ONWARDS.
                          CHIEF OF STAFF.
                BRITISH LIBERATION ARMY.

"They're going to pay, are they?" asked somebody.
"What else can they do?"
"Just came through the letterbox."
"Still trying to reach the Minister."
"Going ahead regardless."
"Every minute counts."
Young turned to Dane. "So Barry was right up to a
point, was he?"
"It's ridiculous. It doesn't fit. I can't understand it."
"I can understand enough of it. Things are what they
seem to be, as they usually are."
"The photograph in the papers showed her left
profile," said Dane, frowning. "Quite likely she never
had any taken full face. That cuts down rather drastically
the number of people who could have known about the
port-wine mark."
"Family, friends, people at work?"
"Can safely be left out of it. If they're at all as I imagine
them, they can't possibly include somebody who'd commit four previous murders just to mislead everyone about

the murder of poor little Pauline Hodges. No, we're left with whoever did the actual killing, and the members of this Committee, and I feel more and more strongly that the latter includes the former."

"Let me see if I understand this." Rather clumsily, Young lit a cigarette. "Possibility One is that the bloody Liberation Army are so to speak bona fide which you're dismissing on aesthetic grounds. Possibility Two is that, some time this morning, MacBean or Varga or whoever it is slips out to a telephone, looks in the book under 'British' and passes on the business about the birthmark just for a joke. Correct?"

"Not really: I could improve on it quite a bit. But it'll do. I agree it's much less plausible than Possibility Three, whereby the murderer, having had it dinned into him by old Barry from the start that the Army can't be taken seriously until it can show some connection with the crimes, has managed to find them and has had a good twelve hours to let them know about the birthmark—not just for a joke. But we won't know exactly why until the finale."

"Possibility Four is the simplest and most plausible of the lot: Royal is and always has been the leader of the Army. I mustn't listen to you any more; you're driving me out of my mind. In the non-technical sense of the phrase, of course."

By nine o'clock that evening such preparations as could be made were complete. The walls of the headquarters were covered with a mosaic of large-scale maps of the Greater London area. On the ground, the largest force of plain-clothes policemen, policewomen and auxiliaries ever assembled in the United Kingdom was standing by in vans, small trucks and similar vehicles, each with its two-way radio tuned to command frequency. All personnel had been thoroughly briefed; strategic grouping had seen to it that the exit routes from any location could be covered within a maximum of fifteen minutes, in most cases much sooner. Helicopter crews had their instructions, vague as these were. Provincial forces were also on alert. Everything that could be done seemed to have been done; yet to Special Commissioner Follett, as he sat waiting with Lambert-Syme, Barry and half a dozen other senior police officials, the outlook appeared gloomy. The enemy held all the initiative; worse, it was hard to believe that the enemy in question *was* the enemy, was in fact responsible for the linked murders, and Follett knew Barry felt the same. But personal belief could count for nothing.

Soon after ten-thirty, coffee and sandwiches were brought in. The commissioner forced himself to eat a little, drink a little: he very much wanted a real drink, but he could not let it be seen by those about him that he wanted one, and if ever a clear head was needed, it was tonight.

At exactly eleven the telephone rang. Barry answered it, switching on a wired-in loudspeaker as he did so.

"Barry here."

"Right, this is the place." A man's voice with a Cockney accent gave rapid details, its amplified tones sounding unpleasantly authoritative. The message ended, "Okay? One man, one car. This time of night he should be able to make it in twenty minutes easy. I hope so, because our bloke's leaving at eleven-thirty either way. All for now—bye-bye."

Follett looked at the section of map that Barry had ringed in pencil.

"Could be worse, Peter, much worse. Crowds and traffic were what I was afraid of. You'd better be away. I'll be here when you get back. Good luck . . .

"Now, gentlemen. Here, here, here . . . here. And here and here. And two men on the heath, though he'd need a tank to get out that way. That's it. Move."

The heath Barry had referred to occupied a considerable segment of the circle he had drawn. It was shown as a tapered oblong strip perhaps a mile and a half long and a third to a half broad; small patches of woodland were indicated on it. Roads ran on either side, converging at both ends. The south-western road adjoined a residential area with side-streets running off it. Near the head of each of these, a man with a walkie-talkie would have concealed himself well before Follett could arrive on the scene. The same would apply to the roads leaving the two ends of the heath. Further off, out of all sight and hearing, vehicles of the task force would soon take up their positions in readiness for a Low-Profile Mobile Surveillance operation. Under LPMS, vehicle A, alerted by a watcher on foot, would follow a suspect for a limited distance before turning off, whereupon vehicle B, alerted in turn by vehicle A, would take on the pursuit, and so on. The procedure was not suited to all traffic conditions, but it stood a chance tonight, thought Barry.

He continued to gaze at the map while, behind him,

his colleagues spoke urgently into telephones and radio-telephones. The pick-up point was half-way along the south-western edge of the heath. Why not the north-eastern edge, where there was a shopping area, pubs, perhaps a cinema, certainly people? Because not far behind it ran a railway line, blocking escape that way.

Barry turned aside. The thing would have to take its chance now.

Peter Follett reached the south-western edge of the heath at 11:21. He forced himself to wait another five minutes to give the force that much more time to position itself. They were uncomfortable minutes.

On the passenger seat beside him stood a stout canvas bag containing the stipulated amount of money in the stipulated denomination and condition. It also contained, expertly hidden, a miniaturised homing cell already transmitting on a low-frequency waveband. What was making Follett uncomfortable was not the cell (which brought him no reassurance either) but the money, something about the money. The second communication from the so-called BLA had demanded a much larger sum than the first, the third and latest the same as the second. Why? They could have asked for a million and would still have had to be paid. As it was, the bag weighed over a hundred pounds, near the limit of what one man could carry for anything more than a short distance—as he himself had already discovered. One man. Carry. The load might indeed be destined to be carried at some stage; but by one man? Was all this complicated operation going to turn out to be the work of one man?

Follett gave it up. He restarted his car and moved round the shallow arc between houses and heath. The grassy slope rose at a gradient that not even a tank could have made short work of. The street lighting was poor, but good enough to illuminate sufficiently what he was looking for. He slowed and picked up his radio-microphone.

"Freddie here."

"Receiving you, Freddie."

"White Morris Marina 1971, NME 946K, parked on heath side. Man standing by passenger door, average build, dark boiler suit, stocking mask—Freddie out."

Follett drew up a few yards from the Marina and rolled down his window. The man approached without hurry. It was impossible to guess at his age, the colour of his hair, anything; and when he spoke he did so with his throat muscles tensed, producing a plummy sound, high-pitched and unnatural.

"Evening, squire. I thought you were never coming. Get out and bring the cash with you."

When he had done as he was told, Follett saw that the other carried a roll of what looked like sacking under his arm.

"I don't like these old police bags," said the odd voice. "Liable to let you down, so I've brought my own. Shifting the cash'll show it is cash and there's about enough of it. You wouldn't really short-change me, though, would you? Come on, give me a hand."

The roll of sacking turned out to be a hessian bag, or

rather a pair of these joined by a broad band of the same material. Both men set to work restowing the bundles of notes.

"Fivers?"

"Yes."

"Lovely."

The task was soon done, but the unknown made no move to pick up his booty. "I must say, these coppers of yours are well trained," he said. "The place must be crawling with them and I haven't noticed a thing."

Just then there came the sound of somebody or something moving in a small clump of trees a dozen yards beyond the Morris.

"What's that?" asked Follett involuntarily. There was no visible movement. What was visible, now that he looked in that direction, was the back of a vehicle. He recognised its tall, squarish shape without being able to identify it.

"Just your nerves, squire," was the answer to his question. "You're all strung up. Relax. Especially for the next half-minute or so."

They waited in silence, the masked man with his back turned to the pavement opposite, while a middle-aged couple went by, giving them an incurious glance.

"Fine. Now a couple more things and I'll be off. Hold your arms away from your sides. That's great."

"You don't think I'd be carrying a gun, do you?" asked Follett, while the other's hands pinched at and patted his clothing.

"No, but you might be carrying a radio, and that

might just make the bit of difference I wouldn't care for. Anyway, you're not. Nice car you've got there."

They moved slowly over to it, ludicrously like (it occurred to Follett) a salesman and a prospective customer in a motor showroom.

"Real nice. Complete with radio, I see. And probably complete with radio I don't see as well." (There was indeed a midget transceiver taped to the underside of the dashboard shelf.) "Seems a pity, but—"

The weird voice tailed off. Its owner reached across the lowered window, let fall a roundish object inside and made at top speed towards the hessian bag. Follett had time to fling himself flat on the grass of the heath before the grenade went off, but the explosion dazed him for a moment. When he looked up, the masked man was disappearing into the nearby clump of trees. Follett struggled to his feet and took a few steps away from the heat radiated by the now fiercely burning car. The flames gave off light as well as heat, enough light for him to see something that filled him with amazement and despair at the same time: a horse and rider mounting the gradient and disappearing beyond its top.

There was no longer any problem about the limitation on the amount of the blackmail payment and consequently on its weight. Follett brushed the thought aside. In a matter of seconds he was having more literally to brush aside people hurrying to the scene of the fire from the houses across the road.

"What happened? Are you all right?"

"Was it a bomb? Was it the IRA?"

"There may be another one—there's another car there."

"Look out!"

"I'm a police officer," shouted Follett. Where the hell were the men from the watching-posts? "There's no more danger. Please get back to your homes."

A man in a raincoat came into view at the double. Follett caught the bulk and the glint of what must be a walkie-talkie clipped to his belt, and hurried towards him. The two met in the middle of the roadway at the edge of the glare from the burning car.

"Commissioner? Are you all right, sir?"

"Yes, yes—get your mobile units to close in on the far side of the heath, keep their distance and look for a man on a horse being picked up by any sort of vehicle. LPMS on the vehicle."

The policeman had had to run nearly 300 yards, some of them uphill, from his position beside a private garage down a neighbouring side-street. He was also alarmed and bewildered. So he said dully, "A man on a horse, sir?"

"Yes! A man on a horse! Get going!"

"Orange F-3 to Control. Freddie's orders. Mobile units—"

Follett searched violently for a cigarette. At its narrowest point, the strip of heath, his glance at the map had told him, was about 600 yards across. In ideal conditions, a horse could touch 30 miles an hour. This horse, carrying the equivalent of a very heavy man across roughish ground, might manage half that: seven yards a second, say. Allowing time for the contact to be made and the load transferred, he could hope for a total of three minutes, possibly more. It seemed an age since that glimpse of the departing rider, but in all probability not more than a couple of minutes had gone by. By now the mobile units must have started to close in. If those calculations were correct, they should have a chance—if, also, they met no traffic problems, and if the opposition had no more tricks up their sleeve. What sort of mind had contrived that horse?

Follett and his companion stood now on the pavement. Several cars had reached the vicinity of the fire or were approaching it.

"They think it's Guy Fawkes night," said the policeman. "Shall I get you some transport, sir? You might like to come along to HQ and follow things from there."

"Yes, I might, on the assumption there's anything to follow."

It was well past closing-time in The Fox and Grapes, a couple of miles away down the road to central London, but the man with the red moustache and the man with the red face still lingered over the fire—an electric one, naturally, crowned with a not very realistic representation of a heap of burning coals.

"What beats me," said the man with the red moustache, "is how he gets them to go along with him. At this stage of the game; easy enough to start with. But this thing's been all over the papers and the telly for days, and he still goes on getting them to go along with him."

"They don't see him," said the other. "They can't."

"You haven't been keeping up with it. They haven't

struggled; nobody's heard anything. He must have a car, he must do it in the car, and they must be getting in of their own free will. How does he do it?"

The man with the red face drained his empty glass. "There's an awful lot of people never look at the papers or the telly. That show where they get blokes to do bloody silly things like milking goats—'Public Projector,' is it? They'd never get me, but they get enough every time."

"They can afford duds and this chap can't. Never gets one, though. Luck of the devil, or—"

"Well, you never think it's going to be you in a thing like that."

"Come on, you two, get going," said a girl's voice. "Unless you want to be locked in for the night."

The speaker was a tall, broad-shouldered girl of 23 named Tessa Noble, barmaid at The Fox for the past year. She was dressed for outdoors and carried a large handbag. The owners respectively of red moustache and red face got to their feet without demur.

"We were just talking about these murders, Tessa," said the latter, moving towards the street door. "What do you think of them?"

"Oh, they don't bother me."

"They should, though. You walking home?"

"It's only just round the corner."

"Where's that boy-friend of yours? Working late?"

"So he said."

"Look, Tessa, why don't you let us come with you? Just as far as your door, mind. Safety in numbers."

"It's out of your way. I'll be all right, honestly."

"Well, if you see anyone you don't like the look of, scream the place down. Fix that in your mind before you start, now. Good night. See you tomorrow."

Tessa Noble walked briskly along the pavement past the hi-fi shop, the place that called itself a boutique, the off-licence. It was a clear night, not cold, but with an occasional sharp eddy of air. Cars droned to and fro almost continuously; a man and a woman were strolling a hundred yards ahead; another couple walked more purposefully by on the other side of the road. So it went as far as the corner of the block. Then Tessa turned off.

Before her lay the downward slope of the side-street, dead straight for 300 yards to the T-junction where she would turn again and within a few paces reach her parents' house. There were a number of cars parked at the kerbs, all of them unlit. Nothing moved. Often at this time, people would be coming out of houses, standing in talk, leading a dog. Not tonight.

As she started down the hill, she felt a warmth rising up the back of her neck and head, while at the same time it was as if that area were being sprayed with fine particles that were neither hot nor cold, but not tepid either. She was always afraid in these circumstances; the wave of murders had given definition to her fear without intensifying it. Some other girls who felt as she did would have at once accepted the friendly offer of the two men at the pub. But that would have been to give in, and Tessa Noble preferred to suffer this fear like her fear of the Underground and of lifts and of heights, rather than give in to it. If she once did, it seemed to her that she would have given in altogether and would find herself incapable of leading a normal life. So, breathing with enforced steadiness, her fists clenched tight, she walked on, briskly as before, not hurrying—that would have been a concession to her fear and was also, as she had found, a sure way to increase it.

When she was half-way to the T-junction, somebody came out of a dark entry between two houses and hurried after her. It was an almost silent progress, because this person's shoes were covered with thick woollen socks. The face was unrecognisable behind a stocking mask. Still there was no movement in the street apart from that of the two figures. The gap between them had closed to a couple of yards when Tessa heard a faint sound and started to turn, but had no chance to do more because her pursuer had closed with her. A left hand, a gloved hand, fastened across her mouth; a right hand, a hand holding a broad, sharply pointed knife, came over her shoulder. The point went through her clothing and her skin, but no further, thanks to that small reaction of hers which had seen to it that the assailant was not quite squarely behind her. And in a moment her strong right hand was gripping the wrist of the knife-hand, her left twisting at the fingers over her mouth.

Tessa kicked backwards and made contact several times, though without effect: the heels of the low shoes she wore to minimise her height had no hardness in them. The struggle continued until Tessa, pushing out-wards at the other's left wrist, managed to drop her head forward, then brought it sharply back. There was a faint yielding sound and a squeal; the attacking hands and arms slackened for a moment; she broke loose and drove her knee up.

"Hey, what's going on? Hold it!"

A man ran from across the street, followed by another; behind them was an open, lighted front door.

"What the hell . . . Are you hurt? There's some blood here."

"It's not mine. I think I got his nose."

"Let's have a look at him."

"Good God!" said Tessa when the mask was pulled off.

"What's the matter? Are you sure you're all right?"

"Oh yes, I'm . . . I'm all right. I feel fine."

The two men looked wordlessly at each other, then at the face that had been uncovered.

CHAPTER FIVE

"It wasn't your fault, Peter," said Barry over a scratch breakfast in the conference room. "Nobody could have thought of that horse."

"Somebody did."

"He'd had days, working it out and picking his location."

"Yes, I know. Conceit, really—not wanting to look a fool whether you deserve to or not."

"We all look like that, the whole committee. Fine time the papers had this morning. My guess is the Minister'll disband us any moment."

Follett, buttering toast, shook his head emphatically. "He'll fight to the death to keep us in being. That's what we're for, to be jeered at: it takes the heat off him. Our Dickie's a cunning one all right."

"I'm afraid I don't—"

"The Committee was his idea, you know. Oh, he let

Charles Paynter put it forward, of course, but Paynter won't forget. One more rung up the ladder for the zealous Lambert-Syme. I've worked with him before, Bill."

"Politicians," said Barry in a heavy voice.

"That equestrian artist would have a future there, wouldn't he? Bold as brass. You pinch a horse and a horse-box from a low-grade stables where there won't be much in the way of security, drive to a place where horses are quite often seen, park the horse-box, take the horse across the road and tie it up, and. . . . And present us with a horse, five people who saw a horse, two people who saw a man getting off a horse, and three people who saw two men putting something heavy into what turns out to have been a stolen taxi. Here he is now. Pack up your troubles in your old kit-bag, Bill, and smile, smile, smile."

Lambert-Syme had entered the room with a buoyant step which he moderated a little as he approached the hunched figures of the two police officials.

"Hallo, you chaps. Bad luck about last night."

Barry was filling a pipe. "We were just saying so to each other."

"I suppose that's an end of the matter?"

"Well . . . the birthmark business shook me. I didn't know what to think. The stabbings and all the South-East rubbish with the letters, all the care taken to leave no traces—the whole thing just didn't go with any sort of bunch of terrorists and that messy shooting at Royal's place. It would have been possible for someone to have found out about the birthmark by nosing about locally; at least, I could never prove it wasn't. But then this horse caper—that was planning. Could be the same sort of mind as decided not to use bombs. So either yes, it's over, and we're left with a little matter of five unsolved murders on our hands, and we keep an eye open for the money turning up, only that horse expert isn't going to be throwing handfuls of cash about this lunchtime at the supermarket. Or . . . I was right the first time, which isn't a lot of satisfaction, is it?"

"What do you really think?" asked Follett. "What do you feel?"

"I'm keeping it to myself, what I feel," said Barry.

> EXTRACT FROM THE PROCEEDINGS OF THE SPE-
> CIAL INVESTIGATORY COMMITTEE, Day 4.
> Present: Lambert-Syme (in the chair),
> Barry, Costello, Dane, Follett, Hender-
> son, Kemp, MacBean, Varga, Young.
>
> *Kemp:* Name of Arthur Johnson, 28. Watch-
> maker's assistant. History of violence and
> mental instability. Girl said he'd been pes-
> tering her for some time. Turned nasty
> one evening when she told him she had a
> regular boy-friend, thanks very much.
> Said all he intended to do was give her a
> fright.
>
> *MacBean:* No doubt he accomplished that, if no
> more.
>
> *Kemp:* Funny you should say that, sir, she
> didn't seem to have turned a hair. Other
> way on, if anything—toned up, almost.

Anyway, it all seems quite straightforward. He'll probably be remanded for a psychiatric report.

Varga: Very probably indeed.

Barry: Not our worry. Crime of imitation.

Costello: Are we quite sure?

Kemp: He was in the pub throughout the material time on two of the evenings in question.

Lambert-Syme: Anybody got anything at all? Mr. Dane?

Dane: Well . . . No.

Henderson: Even the wildest fancy might help us at this stage.

Young: Agreed.

Dane: If you insist. I'm not going to offer any theories or views for the moment, but what I will give you is a prediction. As follows. There will be another murder, probably several. The next victim will be male. The method will not be stabbing: perhaps some form of strangulation, or even a gun. And there'll be some third factor as well.

Follett: What sort of factor?

Dane: Something extra. Something in the spirit of what's gone before and yet not the same. We'll be able to learn from it if we're bright enough.

Barry: [Indistinguishable]

Lambert-Syme: Forgive me—after all we did ask

you to serve here to use your, er,
intuition—but did this come to you in a
dream or . . . ?

Dane: Not in a dream. And now, if you'll
excuse me, I have work to do. Work
connected with our investigation, naturally.

"We'd be bloody fools to pack it in just now we're
winning, Sean," said Ronnie Grainger. "And what's
forty thousand these days? We could ask for a million
next time."

"And get some old elephant to carry away the loot.
God, that was a fine trick with the nag, now. I still can't
make out how you thought of it."

"Thank you, kind sir," said the third man in the room.
"What can go faster than a man and where a car can't?
Stood to reason."

"It came to you awful quick. One moment you were
blathering about hostages and the next you had this all
cut and dried. As if you got it out of a book or something."

"What are you inferring?"

"Easy now, I'm only expressing my amazement at
your genius."

"Stuff all this," said Ronnie Grainger. "Why's he
keeping thirty, this pal of yours?"

"Because he's changing it quick, that's why. We should
think ourselves lucky he's not asking a damn sight more.
Well, I'm off to Liverpool on the noon train the morrow.
They were asking after me in one of the pubs last night.
That's getting too close for comfort. What about you?"

The third man nodded. "Fade for a bit."

"Where?"

"Hereabouts."

"You're crazy."

"I can get the best cover there is. I know someone. And something."

Grainger made a contemptuous noise: "Chicken, the pair of you. I'm carrying on."

"Ah, you'd never manage on your own, Ronnie lad."

"Who says I'm going to stay on my own?"

"On your own or not, you'd get caught. And then they'd offer you a deal: reduced sentence in return for who you were working with. And you'd take it, Ronnie. I'm afraid I find that quite unacceptable."

Ronnie Grainger fell unconscious to the floor because he had been hit over the head from behind. The man Sean strolled across, taking from his pocket a coil of flexible wire. In a short time Grainger was dead.

"Well, he can't have felt a thing, poor wee fellow. As I've told you before, I hate unnecessary suffering."

"Nice easy way of earning an extra twenty thousand quid apiece."

"Indeed. But I'd have done it for nothing, do you know?"

EXTRACT FROM THE PROCEEDINGS OF THE SPE-
CIAL INVESTIGATORY COMMITTEE, Day 5.
Present: Barry, Costello, Dane, Follett,
Henderson, Kemp, MacBean, Varga,
Young.

Follett: It seems Mr. Lambert-Syme has been delayed. I'm sure he wouldn't mind if we made a start without him. Now you've all had a chance to . . . Excuse me. [Here an official entered, conferred briefly with Follett, and left.] Mr. Lambert-Syme is indisposed. He sends us his apologies, and asks me to take the chair at this meeting. Which I was just in the process of doing. Shall we get down to business? Has anyone any comments or questions on these preliminary reports?

Varga: Two victims now. The sickness is spreading.

MacBean: I'm sorry—I thought, according to Dr. Varga, that it is our civilisation that is diseased and that barbarities such as these are signs of resurgent health.

Follett: Could we please have an end to people scoring personal points? This affair is far too serious. Well, Mr. Dane?

Dane: I need hardly point out that both these cases fulfill the prediction I made yesterday. Both victims male. Both strangled. Grainger with wire. Bonello with a scarf. Which is very interesting indeed if you think about it; the fact of strangulation, I mean. And the third factor. Bonello's body had the usual letters attached to it, the rest of the S and a T, plus a complete set of all the previous letters. Grainger had a blackmail note on him in the same handwriting as the previous one. Quite a prediction, wasn't it?

Barry: Really, Mr. Chairman, I—

Dane: I shan't keep you a moment, Chief Superintendent. I just want to know whether these killings could have been the work of the same person.

Barry: They could obviously. Anybody who isn't a fool can see—

Follett: Bill, I—

Barry: Anybody can see from this stuff that Grainger was killed some time in the afternoon and then taken and dumped, and Bonello had only been dead an hour or so when he was found soon after eleven. But they can't be connected. We've got some later information on the Grainger case and the position is this.

Grainger was a petty criminal with a record of violence and theft. One of the local coppers remembers having spotted him near the police station at the time of the Hodges case. There was a bit of a crowd there and he must have picked up the information about the birthmark from one of them. A better brain than his plans it from then on. This ragtime Liberation Army gets its cash and what would it do then? Split up is what it'd do. But Grainger can't be trusted, or the others get greedy, so they knock him off in the only quick, handy, silent, non-messy way they know and dump him with this note as a kind of final V-sign. Oh, we're getting the money together, we've got to, and we'll stand by the phone, but either they won't call us or if they do there'll be nobody there when our man turns up.

So it must be a coincidence that these two men were murdered in roughly the same way. Then why shouldn't it be a coincidence that the Bonello murder was like what Dane—Mr. Dane predicted? If you gentlemen knew more about police work you'd know how likely it is for there to be coincidences. We had a thumping big one right at the start of this business with that A-B-C sequence. And this one's nothing much anyway. Point one: male victim. Bonello had long hair and you can't tell by the way they dress these days and it was dark. Our man goes too far before he realises and has to finish him off. Point two: strangulation. The murderer had tried one kind of knife and found it was unreliable, tried another and likely got some blood on himself. A gun? Whatever you may think, silencers are hard to come by, much harder than just guns themselves, and people tend to bleed when you shoot them quite as much as when you stab them, not over you or your clothes necessarily, but over your car if they're in it at the time or you put them in it. That wraps that up to my satisfaction.

Dane: Point three?

Barry: I was coming to that. What was it? "A feature absent from the previous cases." Pretty wide, isn't it? You might have said Hodges's birthmark was that.

Dane: Can you explain the purpose of reminding us of the earlier letters?

Barry: I can't, no. But it doesn't bother me, not specially.

MacBean: Forgive me, Chief Superintendent, but why are you going to so much trouble to refute the results of, with respect, Mr. Dane's crystal-gazing?

Barry: I'd have thought that was obvious. In an affair like this, with all these, what would you call them?—bizarre elements, it's doubly important that we keep clear heads and stick to hard facts.

MacBean: Yes, it is obvious, of course. Thank you.

Follett: Well, if no one has any further points I'm going to adjourn this session. I'm not sure when we shall be reconvening, but I'll see that word reaches you. Er, I wonder if I could ask you, Dr. Henderson, and you, Dr. Young, to keep the headquarters informed of your whereabouts at all times.

Either of you might be needed in a hurry.
I'm sure you're both used to that. Yes. In
fact, perhaps you'd all be kind enough to
do the same. It's a bother, I know, but it
might help.

Varga: I can't see why you should require me so
rapidly, Commissioner.

Follett: Neither can I at the moment, Dr.
Varga; it's just that one can never be sure.

"One telephone call before we go," said Follett to
Barry a few moments later. "Lambert-Syme."

"Is it anything serious?"

"The messenger said he wasn't told."

Barry lit his pipe and waited. When Follett had
finished he looked troubled.

"Bad, is it?"

"That's what I still don't know, Bill. I met a blank
wall. In the shape of his private secretary, who accepted
that I was who I said I was and everything and told me
in a cheerful voice on the verge of a scream that Mr.
Lambert-Syme was indisposed. In what way? To what
extent? Just indisposed. What do you make of that?"

"Hangover?"

"No, Dickie's never been one for the bottle. Says it
interferes with his womanising."

"He doesn't half go on about that. You'd think nobody
else had ever had it in until he came along. No, it'll be
nothing, Peter. You'd have heard soon enough if it was
anything."

"You're probably right. Let's get on the move."

As they sat side by side in the back of the official car, Barry said, "I didn't much care for MacBean's question about me going on about young Dane's crystal-gazing."

"I wasn't mad about his answer to what you said, either."

"And I'm not bursting with pride over what I said to him in between."

"Oh, I thought it sounded very convincing."

"I hope he did. I should have been ready for him. You were good, though."

"Helped out by Varga. He's been some use at last."

In his flat, Christopher Dane was speaking into the telephone.

"Got that, sweetheart? About eleven. You went to sleep straight away." He looked over his shoulder out of the window and went on more rapidly, "I can't explain now, but you'll have a good laugh when I do. I left after the kids had gone to school. Don't say anything to them. Bye."

He put the instrument in its cradle and breathed deeply. Within seconds the front-door buzzer buzzed, and within not many more he was admitting Follett and Barry.

"I knew it," he said in tones of delight. "Let me have your coats. Tea? Coffee? Drink? No. Well, sit yourselves down. Forgive the elation—it's not often you cast your bread upon the waters and it returns to you in the form of such a thumping great loaf. What price crystal-grazing now, eh? And what price that local copper who recognised Grainger hanging around the station? It was good,

though. You could have fooled me. And I thought the
way you lost your temper about the rubbish I was
talking—full marks for that."

"Thanks," said Barry.

"So you accept my theory? Very much including our
man leaking the birthmark to Grainger and his pals and
thinking up the horse?"

Follett looked severely at Dane. "We don't say we
accept it."

"But you can't afford to ignore it. Right. Of course you
don't *accept* it, or five people, including myself, would
have gone straight from that conference-room to the
cells, wouldn't we?"

"Five people?"

"The obvious four, plus Inspector Kemp. An outsider,
admittedly, but you fuzz are used to spreading your bets,
or you ought to be. And another person, not present this
morning or yesterday for that matter, would either be in
the jug with the rest of us or have become the object of
a very earnest search."

"Royal."

"Before we start," said Dane, sitting on the edge of his
chair, "you might care to know that I spent the whole of
yesterday evening in the company of my wife. The night
too, actually, but all you care about is up to eleven. Ring
her and check—she's always in at this time."

"I will," said Barry. "What did you do, apart from
presumably eat your dinner?"

"Read a book mostly."

Half a minute later, Barry was saying into the telephone, "Mrs. Dane? Police here. We're checking on the

movements of everyone connected with the case your husband's helping with and it's come round to his turn. He says he took you to the pictures last night. What was the film called? . . . I see. Thank you." He rang off and turned to Dane. "According to Mrs. Dane you watched television."

"The book was called *Death Draws the Curtain*."

"She thinks it was *Death Pulls the Curtain*, but we won't quarrel about a what? A verb. All right, that'll keep me quiet for the moment."

"Sort of clears the air, doesn't it? Of course, I might have fixed it up with her just before you came. Did you notice if the receiver was residually warm, as from the grasp of a human hand?"

"Hush," said Barry. "Royal. The Commissioner and I rather like the look of Mr. Royal."

"Chiefly because he has the strongest connections with various *shady* places that could have put him in touch with the Liberation lot. Or is known to have such connections. Mm. Tell me: those summaries or transcripts or minutes of what we all say at those hilarious sessions—are they posted to the Committee members ever, delivered by messenger, anything like that?"

"Not supposed to leave the building. A member could walk out with one, of course."

"Ah. And Royal wasn't there when I made my famous prediction. So how did he know about it? It's most annoying, because I had my eye on him too."

Follett said unhappily, "Somebody else on the Committee . . . told him."

"Oh no! One's hard enough to believe in, but two! It

can't be. Look at the motive behind all this. I don't mean the particular motive, the immediate one, which in Royal's case might be that his popularity was falling off, so a new way of attracting attention was called for."

"In that case he must intend to be caught."

"In his own good time, which raises another . . . But to go back to Royal's popularity for a moment—it isn't falling off. I had no trouble establishing that in the last year his record sales have gone up faster than ever before. Now the motive again, the real, fundamental, perhaps unconscious or half-conscious drive. It's power, isn't it? You behave like a god, striking down your victims as you please, without hatred, according to your own arbitrary pattern, defying all the ingenuity and imagination of mere mortals until the moment comes, appointed by you and you only, when you reveal yourself and the world gasps in awe. Well, the world's gasping at Royal already, though he might feel it's the wrong sort of gasp, I suppose. But let's just run through the others.

"Varga—now there's a man if I ever saw one who's cross because he isn't God. And off his head, too, as Quintin Young will tell you. Costello—aren't all lawyers keen on power, especially prosecuting ones? I tried to find out what his prospects were, becoming a judge and so on, but I didn't get anywhere much. Tight-mouthed lot, our learned friends. Kemp—a closed book and probably not worth opening. MacBean—now there's the chap I really like the look of from this point of view. Tremendously ambitious and with no hope of any real advancement. I know two or three political journalists and they agree he's in a cleft stick. Stop calling for the rope and he loses his notoriety, his distinction; go on calling for the rope and he stays out of office indefinitely. And some would say that just being interested in the rope made you interested in death. Or else callous about it.

"Now; if you go along with the power theory you have to rule out any notion of a confederate. That sort of power is unshareable by definition. It's one individual against all the rest; one individual and a chum or two against all the rest is too feeble. A god doesn't need human aid. Well, what do you say?"

Follett lit a cigarette. "I say I think I'll take that drink."

"Very sensible."

While he poured the drinks, Dane went on half-abstractedly:

"Wonderful arrogance to follow my prediction. No mystery there. But those damn letters . . . South-East . . . no idea. And the locations . . . surely significant. To get first Bonello and then his body from his neighbourhood to Plaistow Station meant a drive of seven or eight miles. But the map shows nothing. Just a jagged line. Imagine it dotted. Columbus's voyage. The route of the procession. Here we are—cheers. I don't envy you two. You can't arrest anyone, because you haven't got any evidence. You can't start a surveillance programme, because that would reach the Press in no time, and you'd—"

"Oh yes we can," said Barry. "Start a surveillance programme. Only it's not called that: it's called a protection programme. The police have fresh evidence to suggest that the recent attack on Benedict Royal may be the first of a series and have therefore rhubarb rhubarb."

"I thought you hadn't got the men."

"That was two days ago. I'll have to get Lambert-Syme's authorisation first. Can I . . . ?"

While Barry dialled and waited, Dane said to Follett, "That'll stop the murders but it won't catch the murderer. And how long are you going to keep up your so-called protection? A year? Our chap would be perfectly happy to sit around knitting until he's free to take another crack. Meanwhile your only hope is that you can somehow reduce your five to one, whom you consider arresting, not exactly egged on by the horrible suspicion that that clever 'tec-yarn fellow has been feeding you a lot of hogwash and the real murderer's somebody you've never. . . ."

"Mr. Lambert-Syme? Bill Barry. Look, something's come up. I want your authority to put round-the-clock police protection on Royal, Costello, MacBean, Varga and Kemp. Straight away. I'll explain later—the point is—What? Who's that? Who? Where is he? Well, find out, fast, and give him that message. Get him to ring me at. . . . No, I'll ring you later. Now get going."

Barry turned from the telephone to the other two.

"Some underling who ought to be sweeping the floors and making the tea by the sound of him. Let's be away, Peter."

"The police are about to follow up their lead," said Dane, grinning.

"Lead?" growled Barry. "Lead? I'd call it something to do."

"At least it's that," said Follett.

"Yeah." Barry got up and considered. "I think Costello first."

"You think he's the likeliest?"

"No, but he may be the simplest. Can I . . . ?"

"By all means. I shouldn't hope for too much there, though."

"I'm not hoping for anything."

Barry dialled, waited, spoke briefly and rang off.

"He's there and ready to receive us."

As the policemen moved towards the door, Dane said brightly, "Is it all right if I come along?"

"No, sir," said Barry. "I know it's always all right for your James Fenton bloke to come along, but this is different."

"We hope," said Follett.

"Well, thank you very much for your advice, Mr. Dane. And the drink."

"Any time, Detective Chief Superintendent."

Left alone, Dane spent a little while chuckling and shaking his head in the way he had. Then he put on his overcoat and left the flat.

"No, the significance doesn't escape me, gentlemen. Every evening you mention, and many previous ones, I've dined early at my club, returned here, spent the evening reading, talking to my wife, even working. Isn't that right, my dear?"

"Absolutely right. Absolutely right."

"And you haven't gone out after arriving home?"

"No."

"And you've seen nobody? Apart from Lady Costello?"

"No."

"And you've nothing to add to that? No other supporting evidence of any kind?"

"No."

"I see, sir. Thank you. May I use your telephone?"

"Certainly. Through the arch and on the left."

Embarrassed and illogically ashamed, Follett stared in the direction of a large portrait of a nineteenth-century Lord Chancellor. Costello watched him with a sad smile before starting to talk about the subject of the painting. Behind them, the neck of a bottle clunked on to a glass and liquor was noisily poured.

"He should be in his flat but he isn't," said Barry, returning. "Oh, excuse me, Sir Neil. He may have gone to his constituency."

"Are you referring to Mr. MacBean? Because it occurs to me now that he left after the meeting this morning in as much of a hurry as I've seen anybody outside a railway station. A man normally so deliberate in his movements."

"Missed him by hours and hours." The porter at the block of flats diffused satisfaction. "Yes, he took off, oh, two-thirty? Carrying a couple of suitcases. I asked him if he wanted a hand and he didn't take a blind bit of notice. Funny."

"Did he seem upset?" asked Barry.

"Couldn't say."

"Did he have a car waiting? A taxi?"

"No idea, sir. But I can tell you he don't run a car of his own."

"Thank you for being so helpful."

In the street, Barry said, "We need peace and quiet, Scotch, telephones and a couple of helpers who'll keep their mouths shut."

"My room at the Yard has got all of those."

"We're lousy actors, Peter, you and I," said Barry later. "He twigged right away at the Committee."

"What more could we have done? Beaten Dane to a pulp to show how ridiculous we thought his theory was?"

"Let's see what we've got. He's not anywhere he usually goes. Not in his constituency or expected there. Probably still in the country, quite possibly still in London. But he's done a bunk all right. People like MacBean don't forget things like being told to notify their whereabouts."

"We'll soon find him, Bill. That amnesia idea of yours was brilliant."

"I quite care for your one about him being in danger from the mass killer who's been terrorising, et cetera. By tomorrow morning everyone'll be looking for him."

"People like MacBean. Do people like MacBean run away?"

"Oh, now and then. What bothers me is what we do with him when we've found him."

"We'll cross that bridge when we come to it. By the way, has anybody ever tried crossing a bridge before they come to it? Come on, knock that back. One more call and we can go and eat."

"You eat. I'll sleep."

*   *   *

In his study that evening, Henry Addams, who had been sitting at his table without moving for several minutes, raised his head with a jerk, as if he had heard his name called in an unfamiliar voice. He looked briefly round the interior of the hut, then at the scrap-book that lay open before him. Reading with great speed, he moved back through it to its first page. After that, he rose to his feet so hastily that he upset his chair, made a quick inspection of the wall-map (now clustered with paper flags) and rummaged through the contents of the chest of drawers with the urgency of a man who has lost something valuable. If such was the case, his search was unrewarded. When it was over, he stood looking at the wall, and trembling violently. At last, he left the hut, leaving it unlocked behind him for the first time since it was built, and made his way, with much hesitation and many glances about him, to the back door of the house. In the same fashion he entered the sitting-room. His wife smiled at him from her chair.

"Finished your work, dear, have you? You're early."

"Yes . . . Tell me, have there been some horrible murders committed in London recently?"

"You know there have, dear. They've been in the paper and on the television and we've talked about them. You've been very interested in them, haven't you?"

"Yes. Yes, I have. I must go out now."

"Oh, you don't want to do that, dear, not on a nasty cold night like this, not with your cough and everything."

"I must go. There's something I have to . . . buy."

"Well, you won't find many shops open at this time. Are you all right, dear?"

"Yes. Thank you. I'm all right."

"You sound funny. Look, why don't you go on your bike? Much quicker."

"My . . . Where is it?"

"Where it always is, silly. Under the shelter by the coal-bin."

"Yes. Well . . . good-bye."

After some delay, Henry Addams found his bicycle, mounted it and pedalled in the direction where he could see most lights. Inquiries from pedestrians brought him to the local police station, a building he passed at least ten times a week. What he said there ended eventually in his being confronted by a rather cross-looking young man in a dinner-jacket who said he was a doctor. Three other men, two of them in uniform, were there too. The room was small and under-furnished, but comfortably warm.

"You say you may have committed these murders," said the doctor. "Why? What makes you think so?"

"All the stuff I showed the police in that shed thing, the books and the bits from the papers and the map with the flags on it. And that knife they found."

"No blood on it that I could see," said one of the other men. "But we won't know for certain until tomorrow."

"I must have cleaned it."

The doctor swept the air with his hand. "Never mind that for now. Just think hard, Mr. Addams. Have you any memory at all, even the vaguest and faintest memory, of yourself doing anything, being anywhere, seeing anything that has to do with . . . stabbing or strangling people?"

"I've no need to, doctor. Think hard, that is. I've already done that and there's nothing. A complete blank, like with everything else."

"You do mean everything else?"

"Yes. I found I was sitting in that shed. . . . But I've told you it all before."

"Tell us again," said the other man who had spoken.

"I found myself sitting there, quite clear in the head, in full possession of my faculties, but not knowing who I was or where I was or how I'd got there or anything else. I realise I must have been born, been to school, grown up and that, only I can't remember where or . . . My . . . wife knew my name, of course. Is she all right?"

"There's a policewoman with her; she's being looked after."

"It's as if I came into existence for the first time, what, two hours ago?"

One of the men in uniform said matter-of-factly, "We all live in a big city, don't we? What's it called?"

"London."

"How do you know?"

"I saw it on the map."

"That was quick."

"Don't try and trap him, Inspector," said the doctor sharply. "I can tell you what we've got here. It's pretty rare, I've never seen a case before, but it's been fully described. Transient total global amnesia."

"I get it, doctor. You mean he's forgotten everything."

"Well . . . broadly, yes."

"He seems to be able to speak quite well."

"Mentally and emotionally he's normal."

"So according to you we can let him go?"

"Don't let me go, for God's sake," shouted Henry Addams. "Keep me locked up so I can't do any more of these terrible things."

"Don't worry, sir, we don't run any risks in a matter of this kind. However remote they are."

"Mr. Royal is resting and can't be disturbed."

"I see. And you're Mr. . . . ?"

"Mannheim. I'm his manager."

"Should you be up and about so soon after your accident, Mr. Mannheim?" asked Barry. "You don't look at all well."

"I'm all right. Come in, please."

Mannheim led Barry and Follett into what was no doubt a drawing-room with black-and-white tiles on the walls as well as the floor. Upon shooing motions and noises from Mannheim, various strangely clad young persons went out by a further doorway between miniature Ionic columns.

"Can't you tell me what this is all about? We're in a bit of a rush here, because Mr. Royal and I have to leave for a concert very soon."

"I see," said Barry again, mechanically this time. "The thing is, Mr. Mannheim, we think Mr. Royal may be in danger—further danger, that is. He's being put under police protection. We've reason to believe somebody's been shadowing him for some days. Some nights especially. We were going to ask him to say what his movements have been these past few evenings."

"Oh, well I can answer that. He's been with me. Every evening."

"And where were the two of you? Every evening."

"That's confidential, I'm afraid, Inspector, because there's business interests involved. We've been engaged in some protracted commercial negotiations of a confidential nature. Him and me."

"You're talking to two people who it's their stock-in-trade to be confidential, Mr. Mannheim. Where did these negotiations take place?"

"I could tell you exactly if I was allowed to, Inspector, but I'm not. Mr. Royal's strict instructions. Nobody gets to know, not even Scotland Yard. And I don't think I believe quite that much in this shadowing. I think you're trying to—"

Mannheim stopped speaking for the good reason that, from some upper floor, there came at that moment the sound of a firearm being discharged.

CHAPTER SIX

Mannheim was the first to move. He was half-way up the curving staircase before Barry and Follett had reached its foot. A confusion of voices could be heard from a room at the far end of the landing. In that room, two people faced each other: Benedict Royal, who was holding in his left hand a short-barrelled pistol and in his right hand his upper left arm which was exuding blood; and a weeping girl with her hands over her face.

"Good evening, gentlemen," said Royal in a remarkably steady voice. "I'm afraid you're just too late for the action, but it's most considerate of you to be on hand. This silly cow—It's all right, Marty: only a scratch. As I was saying, this foolish young lady took a shot at me. Name of Karen Priest, by the way. I tell her she doesn't live here any more and she blazes away like it's a fairground. But you'd have to be thought-readers to be here because of her. Thanks, Marty."

Mannheim had helped Royal off with his dressing-gown and now set about attending to the wound, which was indeed shallow.

Barry answered the implied question. "As I was telling Mr. Mannheim, we'd come to the conclusion you were in danger, which is what it looks like, doesn't it? We got evidence that someone's been following you, so we called to inquire about your movements, but it seems that's a waste of time."

"It seems that way from here, too."

"Anyhow, I'm arranging police protection for you among others. It won't guard against this sort of thing, but that's your—"

"I told you before, I don't want police protection."

"The situation was different then, sir. May I use your telephone?"

Royal moved his head in the direction of a green instrument on the bedside table.

"Sorry I can't help you with your inquiries," he said. "Of course, you could try arresting me."

"We will as soon as we can prove you've committed a crime," said Follett, who by now had managed to reduce Karen Priest to some sort of calm.

"You do that. This protection. What'll it mean?"

"A man outside the door and another patrolling."

"Two men won't be much use where I'm going tonight."

"Are you sure you're fit, Benedict?" asked Mannheim anxiously, binding Royal's arm.

"Yeah, I'm fine. At the moment. When I get to the concert I'll be set up like Bobby Kennedy."

Follett spoke with confidence. "We're not expecting any added danger in those circumstances."

"You know a lot, Commissioner, don't you? And yet it doesn't seem to do you any good. Still as far from catching that murderer as ever."

"We're much closer than we were a couple of days ago."

"I bet you're not as close to him as I am. What do you think I've been up to while the rest of you have been talking your heads off? Investigating. Asking questions. And getting answers."

"What sort of answers?"

"By tomorrow I'll have enough for you to be able to get him. In the meantime you can do me a favour and get rid of this slut for me. Just out of the house: I don't want her charged."

"Oh, but I do."

"You heard what he said." Mannheim glared at Follett.

"Yes. However, this appears to be a case of assault with a deadly weapon, and the police are constantly charging people for things like that."

"Sounds reasonable," said Royal, shrugging his shoulders.

"You can't let them, Benedict!"

"I can't stop them, can I? Anyway, do her good."

Barry came bustling over. "Got him at last," he said to Follett. "And given the order. There should be a car up here in five minutes."

"I can hardly wait," said Royal.

RELEVANT PORTIONS OF INTERROGATION OF
    KAREN ELIZABETH PRIEST

You can't deny you fired those shots?

Of course not. There was only the two of us
    there, me and him.

Where did you get the gun?

It's his, he keeps it in the drawer of his bedside
    table.

What happened?

He told me to get out and I said for good and he
    said yes for good and I said why and he
    said because you're a [erased] and I knew
    the gun was there so I just took it and shot
    him.

Were you trying to kill him?

Not specially. I nearly missed him anyway
    didn't I? I wanted to show I was angry, I
    wanted to show I've got feelings. He
    doesn't think I've got any but I have.
    [Pause] Sorry.

Did you plan to shoot Mr. Royal?

I told you, he told me to get out and I just took
    the gun. I've got feelings but he doesn't
    think so. He doesn't think any girls have
    got feelings. He's too good for them, he
    thinks. He just uses them. You know
    where he goes with Marty these nights?

[After consultation] *Tell us about it.*

They make out it's some fantastic business deal
    but it's a long time coming. I know what it
    is really. He goes somewhere where it

turns him on, somewhere kinky. He needs that because girls, just girls aren't really any good to him. I don't know whether that Marty goes with him or not but he'd say anything to cover up for him.

It's not just another chick because that's all right. But kinky stuff isn't all right so he gets Marty to say they've been together at these business people's place.

What do you mean by kinky stuff?

I don't know. Whips. Funny clothes. He's never asked me to do any of it so it must be a bit far out.

Has he ever said anything to you or has anybody else said anything that gave you what shall we say any solid reason to think that he goes in for such activities?

No, I just feel it.

Thank you. That'll be all for the moment.

What'll happen to me now?

[After consultation] *You'll probably be remanded in custody for a—*

What?

I shouldn't worry too much if I were you.

Oh thanks.

"Dr. Varga?"

"Yes, what is it?"

"By an order of the Ministry of Domestic Affairs, sir, you're under police protection all round the clock and wherever you go."

"You're joking, my good fellow."

"No, sir. Would you like to see the order?"

"Eventually the idiots have done as I asked. Very well. Will the Ministry of Domestic Affairs object if I take this young lady into my house?"

"I shouldn't think so, sir, would you?"

"All round the clock. When will you sleep? I suppose when you feel inclined."

"No, sir, when we go off duty. There are more than two officers in our local Force, you see. We find it's easier that way. . . . Good night, sir."

"Nice bloke, that," said the second constable a moment later. "Really wins you round straight off."

"That girl must have funny tastes. Good-looking, too."

Varga conducted the girl, one Nora Selby, to his sitting-room on the first floor of the house. With the strains of Mahler's First Symphony emanating softly from his cassette recorder, he poured drinks for the two of them and settled down next to Nora on the black simulated-leather couch. After sociometrical theory, he stopped talking.

"No," said Nora quite soon.

"Come on, what's the harm?"

"How can I tell? Probably there wouldn't be any, but I want more than just no harm. And that's the best I could hope for with someone I know as little as I know you."

"You must have roses and a French dinner?"

"Well, they'd be better than nothing, but I don't operate your way."

"Why did you agree to come with me here? Are you a child?"

"I'd read about you, and I recognized you, and I thought it might be interesting to find out a bit about what you were like."

"You were saying you don't know me."

"I didn't mean. . . . I know a bit and I'm finding out more all the time."

It would have taken a less sensitive man than Varga to miss the coldness in Nora's tone. She might have been frightened if she could have seen the expression on his face as he crossed to the window. Looking down in the direction of the police car, he said:

"Ironical to be given this protection."

"You didn't explain about that. Why do you need guarding?"

"In fact this isn't true, although the police might believe so. I'll let you know the real story, which I've told nobody else. These murders we're hearing of all the time. I committed them." He turned and faced Nora, his eyes dilated. "I did them."

"You did? What for?"

"To prove my power. To show the world it's made of fools."

"Why are you telling me this?"

"If you like, so as to boast, and to do so without any risk, because if you tell anyone I'll simply make a denial. I've covered my traces. I can't be caught. Aren't you frightened?"

"With those men out there I wouldn't be even if I

believed you, and I don't. You're just trying to take it out on me for not falling into your arms just now."

"I am the murderer for whom thousands of police are searching!"

"I'm sorry for you. You're mad."

"*You* are mad. You and the others. I am sane."

Nora Selby picked up her coat and left. Varga watched intently as she came into view below him, walked through the garden gateway and passed the police car without a glance. He did not relax; he continued to stare out of the window and began beating the flat of his hand on the sill.

"I am sane," he said in a casual tone. "I am sane."

"Give him a ring," said Follett.

"Right. Here we are. . . . They say retirement's wonderful, don't they? I wonder what it's like. Incidentally, how do we explain why we aren't guarding Young and Henderson and you and me?"

"We don't."

"That's the answer. . . . Dr. Young? It's Barry here, doctor. Something's come up in your department. Probably nothing in it, but we'd better check. The coppers down Bow way are holding a fellow called Henry Addams who says he's lost his memory and may have done the murders: he's got a hut full of Press cuttings about them and a map with the locations marked and God knows what. All his memory. They've had the local shrink on to him. Yes, he says. . . . 'Transient total global amnesia.' Sounds rather grand, doesn't it? Oh?

Well, if you would. . . . There'll be someone here. Probably me. Oh yes. . . ."

Barry described the whereabouts of the police station involved and rang off. He looked round the conference room with a hostile eye.

Follett asked, "Going tonight, is he?"

"On his way. I'm getting to hate this bloody set-up. Pointless natter half the time and useless work the other half. He said that amnesia thing's very grand indeed: I'd no idea how grand. What did he mean? Well, they're all being so-called protected now. Except MacBean, of course. What have we got? Three blokes with alibis that aren't alibis, Kemp being checked, and we'll get after Varga tomorrow. It isn't boring; you can say that."

"You can indeed. Any moment a telephone'll ring here or next door and tell us there's been another."

"Before it does, I'd better warn them to expect Young."

"Now, this shouldn't take very long," said Young genially, facing Addams in the otherwise empty interview-room. "You came to yourself as you put it, and found you couldn't remember anything at all about yourself, your name, your job, your whole life. Is that right?"

"Well, I know my name now, and I've found out some other things. And just before you came I found I could remember being a child."

"Ah, that's interesting. How old a child?"

"Not very old. Five or six perhaps. Kids' clothes and toys. I wouldn't know how to speak else, would I?"

"Just relax, Mr. Addams: you've nothing to worry

about. There's a lot that can be done for you. After all, your intelligence is unimpaired, isn't it?"

"I don't know. I seem to be able to think all right."

"Steady. Have a cigarette."

"Thank you."

"It's a rotten night, isn't it? I gather you live some distance away. Did you walk it or come by bus?"

"On my bicycle."

"I see." Young produced his wallet and from it his driving licence. "Look at this. What is it?"

"It's . . . it's a sort of official form, isn't it?"

"Correct. You must have been a very precocious five- or six-year-old, Mr. Addams. One who by that age had learnt the meaning of phrases like 'your intelligence is unimpaired,' how to smoke a cigarette, how to ride a bike through traffic, and what an official form is."

"I think I can remember being nine or ten."

"And nineteen and twenty-nine and thirty-nine. You know, writers really should be more responsible. They put all sorts of silly ideas into people's heads. Split personality is one. And total amnesia is another. The only conceivable cause of that would be extremely severe brain-damage, from disease or a blow on the head—so severe as to turn you into a helpless vegetable. Which you're very far from being. What you are is nothing much out of the way: a rather solitary man who's become fascinated with violent crime. No more abnormal, really, than a chap who likes reading about explorers or pirates. We all have our secret lives and our fantasies, and you took yours a little further than most of us do. That's all."

Henry Addams had his head in his hands.

"There's nothing to be ashamed of," said Young, "and nothing to be frightened of. I'll cook up a story for the police."

He was as good as his word. Before leaving, he explained to a bemused inspector that, by the use of certain semantic key-terms pre-selected to trigger off subliminal responses, he had by-passed Addams's traumatic block and liquidated his amnesia. "He's perfectly harmless. Give him a few minutes and then get someone to take him home. Oh, and if I were you I'd think about finding another local head-doctor. The one you've been using doesn't know his job. That's right. And you can quote me."

In the interview-room, Henry Addams raised his head, glanced cautiously to and fro, and laughed silently.

Finding that his return journey virtually took him past the Ministry, and feeling too in need of a measure of congenial company (the encounter with Addams had lowered his spirits), Young decided to make his report in person. The headquarters room was as busy as he had ever seen it; Barry seemed positively animated, something to be taken as a sign of extreme crisis.

"Well?" he demanded of Young.

"Nothing. A crank. I told the police to send him home."

"Was that wise? I suppose it was. You'd know. I've stopped being able to tell the difference between what's wise and what isn't."

"Another killing?"

"No, that's just what it's not. Came through while you

were in the lift, I should think—the coppers have got a fellow with a lump on his nut the size of an egg. One of ours, though: letter R and part of another R pinned to him. Conscious but confused. Alive, anyway. Bungled job. Stratford Station he was found, not much over a mile from where you've just been." Barry was struggling into his overcoat. "I'm on my way over there. Peter'll fill you in. Oh, and thanks for doing your stuff. I've forgotten my manners too. Where's Lambert-Syme? I can't wait for him."

With Barry's departure, relative calm supervened. Follett came up.

"Good to see you, Quintin. Doubly good to see you—I can't think why we didn't get hold of you long ago. If ever there was a case that needed a fresh mind, this is, as they say, it. Let me tell you what's happened in the last few hours."

Young heard him out. Then he said, "A very strange tale."

"Tale is right. Told not by an idiot, I hope, but strongly influenced by a teller of tales. I keep expecting James Fenton to walk in and solve everything. Do you think we're mad? In a fairly loose sense of the term."

"Any explanation that fitted these facts would have to be a little out of the ordinary. And there's logic, too. If Dane's right in saying the chap wants to be caught in the end, he'd also not want to be caught before the end, and being in a position to keep bang up to date with the investigation would be the best possible insurance against that. But MacBean—hard to believe it's got to be him."

"It hasn't quite got to be him, Quintin. Not yet. The police squads weren't all on until about half an hour ago. A bit more: they got to Dane at 10:51."

"Dane too."

"Naturally."

"Why so late?"

"Walking the streets lost in thought, according to him. Excuse me. Ah, Dickie!"

"Good evening, gentlemen," said Lambert-Syme, approaching. "I'd have been here sooner if my damn fool of a driver hadn't got himself lost. Not used to walking—no taxis, of course. Now, what have we here?"

"Are you all right, Dickie?" asked Young. "You don't look at all well."

This was true. Lambert-Syme's normally rubicund face was pale, his forehead shone with sweat and he swallowed every few seconds. "I must have picked up some sort of bug."

"You'd better let me—"

"No, no, I'm all right. We must get on. What's the situation?"

Follett outlined it, ending with, "So we're very interested in the time element."

"There's not a hell of a lot else to be interested in." Young looked thoughtful. "If this chap was out any length of time, he literally won't know what hit him."

"Telephone, Commissioner," called a voice.

Follett hurried away. Lambert-Syme said,

"As with that Mannheim character. Amnesia keeps cropping up in this thing."

"Indeed it does. The period lost is roughly propor-
tional to the period of unconsciousness."

"It comes back eventually, does it?"

"No, never."

"Just as well, I suppose," said Lambert-Syme, yawn-
ing hugely. "Well, Quintin, what brings you here at such
an hour?"

By the time Young had told his Addams story, Follett
had rejoined them.

"Confirmed—the letter fits. And you were right, of
course, Quintin. He's lost the whole day and he's pretty
patchy on a good deal of stuff before that. And the
options are open again. He left work at his usual time,
soon after six, and didn't arrive home; usual time for
that, about twenty to seven. He has a seven-minutes or
so walk from his bus-stop. That's thumbing your nose,
isn't it? Imagine the daring of an attack in the middle of
Islington at that time of the evening."

"Or the desperation," said Lambert-Syme.

In his flat, Christopher Dane looked at his watch and
turned the radio on. Quite soon a voice was saying,

"And that's the end of Midnight Journey—hope you
enjoyed the trip. Now, before we close down, the news
summary. The generals' coup in the Caribbean republic
of Haiti. It's claimed that resistance is confined to a few
outlying areas and Port-au-Prince, the capital, has been
quiet for the last twenty-four hours. The Reign of Terror
murders. Colin Harding, aged twenty-eight, was attacked early tonight in Islington. Although he escaped
serious injury, police are treating the case as a further

strike in the series of crimes that have shocked the entire world. Britain's trade deficit last month was the worst—"

Dane switched off and got to his feet in excitement or agitation. "Escaped serious injury," he muttered several times over with varying stresses. "Mucked it, by God. Mucked it." He strode to his desk and picked up a pad on which was written:

1. Folie à deux
2. He must be ill
3. Bodies moved
4. Fenton's theory
5. More than one kind of power
(and added to it)
6. Getting careless?

The group in the headquarters room was about to break up for the night.

"So here's the final score," said Barry, rubbing his eyes. "Kemp seems clear. Peter and I were at Royal's place just after 7:30. If Harding was right about where he recovered consciousness, and we gather there's no reason to suppose he wasn't, Royal would have had to drive a total of over ten miles from Islington to Stratford, drop Harding off, and then drive a bit further across to Regent's Park, all in about three-quarters of an hour. I don't say it can't be done, even at that time of the evening, but the point is he needn't have done it, because he couldn't have known we were going to drop in, so he's low in the running. Costello was working at home, which is rather convenient for him. Varga refuses to say where he was, refuses at the top of his voice. MacBean's still the obvious favourite."

"And where do I come?" asked Lambert-Syme with a slight grin.

"Nowhere, sir. Somebody who sounded just like somebody on the *Evening Chronicle*, with typewriters going on in the background—good fun setting it up, it was—anyway, a policewoman phoned your social secretary and said they were doing a feature on the private lives of public men, and it turned out, what with receptions and embassy dinners and the rest of it, you haven't had any what you'd call private life for quite a time."

Young broke in, "You've left out thriller novelist Christopher Dane. The man who put this idea into our heads."

"Not a bad alibi for Bonello. And if policemen are allowed hunches, mine is he's in the clear. Anybody else?"

"You're probably right up to a point," said Young. "Policemen always are up to a point, according to Dane. Anyway, since he was brought into this, his hunch-production rate has been pretty fair in terms of quantity. Not so much in quality. One of his major hunches is wrong. That's my hunch."

"Which of his hunches?" asked Lambert-Syme.

"I'm not letting on for the moment. Dane would be quite shocked if I did."

Something over 12 hours later, at 1:35 P.M. in fact, Fergus MacBean sat in a small and rather flashy hotel bedroom off Buckingham Palace Road. He was reading with close attention a newspaper account of the assault on Colin Harding. When he had finished, he glanced briefly at two other front-page stories. One referred to the current Royal tour of Indonesia, the other to "an action-packed day" for the Prime Minister: a working lunch at 10 Downing Street with trade union leaders followed by the opening of a "crucial" debate on employment in the House of Commons. Seemingly deep in thought, MacBean crossed to the dressing-table. Here there lay a sheet-map of the Greater London area and an opened book of larger scale maps, also, among other papers, a tracing that consisted of a single irregular line. After more thought, he turned the book-map to another page and glanced to and fro between it and the tracing. Then, abruptly, he folded the tracing, put it in his pocket and started for the door, which at that moment was knocked on from the outside.

"Who is it?"

"Police."

MacBean hesitated. He looked over his shoulder at the window, where a small balcony and a short drop provided an easy exit-route. But in a moment he turned to the door again. "Come in."

A plain-clothes man and a uniformed constable entered. The former referred briefly to a photograph.

"Mr. MacBean?"

"Yes?"

"Will you come with us, sir? Detective Chief Superintendent Barry would like to ask you some questions."

"And I should like to answer them." MacBean consulted his watch. "I also have some information for him of the greatest urgency. Take me to him at once."

"What about your luggage, sir?"

"There's no time. I said at once."

MacBean sat in the back of the police car with the plain-clothes officer beside him. "Please drive as fast as possible. This is a matter of life and death."

The other turned briefly. "Life and death comes up on the roads all the time, sir. The traffic's heavy today, but we'll make the best speed we can."

After a pause, MacBean asked conversationally, "How did you find me?"

"One of the men on the desk recognised you when you came back from wherever you went this morning, sir, even though you were wearing the glasses and so on."

"Really? I had no idea my face was as well known as that."

"It seems he's a kind of fan of yours, sir." The plain-clothes man spoke with almost imperceptible distaste. "Been to your meetings."

"No doubt his intentions were good."

At Headquarters Barry was on the telephone. He took in MacBean's arrival and soon finished his conversation.

"Superintendent. . . ."

"One moment, sir, if I may."

MacBean waited, moving only to look at his watch, while Barry gave instructions to a uniformed officer. It was not long before those too were completed.

"Well, Mr. MacBean, what have you been up to?"

"Among other things, avoiding arrest. But the other

things are much more important. I believe I have established that the next and final victim of this chain of murders is to be the Prime Minister."

After less than a second, Barry said, "Your reasons?"

MacBean handed over his tracing. "There must be significance in the selection of the places where the bodies have been found. The crosses here represent those seven places. The line joining them corresponds to the direct route between Downing Street and the Central Lobby of the House. The angles and the proportionate distances are the same."

"Number Ten being the first cross, bottom left?"

"Yes."

"That isn't the PM's normal route to the Lobby, is it?"

"No, but it's the one he's using today."

"I'll have it checked."

"Superintendent, you have no time to check. You must act immediately. The time is 2:14. At any moment the Prime Minister will leave Downing Street on his way to the Lobby, where by unbreakable tradition he must present himself at exactly 2:30. And at any moment . . ."

MacBean stopped speaking when Barry handed the tracing, with explanations, to a plain-clothes policeman.

"It'll only take a moment, sir," he said soothingly.

"A moment may be too long. Telephone Downing Street and warn him to stay where he is."

"You must see that's impossible."

"If you won't, I will."

"No, sir." Barry was firm. "Now, have you anything else to go on?"

"These dreadful events must issue in a climax. You can't think they were meant simply to cease. What better climax than the public assassination of the second most important person in the nation?—the most important person of all is on the other side of the world at this moment, thank God." Although he was trembling visibly, MacBean's voice remained steady. "The whole psychology of—"

"But a public assassination would be certain to . . ." Barry stopped speaking.

"To lead to the instant apprehension of the assassin. Of course. Haven't we all agreed that this lunatic wants nothing better?"

"It fits, sir," said a new voice.

"How exactly?"

"I couldn't tell you that without a full blow-up, sir. But . . . pretty exactly."

"Thank you." Barry stared at MacBean. "Coincidence. Coincidence and a bit of amateur psychology."

"Are you going to do nothing, Superintendent?"

"No, I'm going to do something, sir. I'm going to inform the Prime Minister and follow whatever orders he gives. And check the security arrangements at the House."

"When? Next week?"

"No, sir. Now."

"Take me with you. I know my way round the place."

Barry nodded and the two started for the door.

On his second police-assisted journey within an hour, MacBean again sat at the back. Barry was beside him, with a plain-clothes man in front and a uniformed sergeant driving. The car hurried down Whitehall.

"What exactly happens at two-thirty?" asked Barry.

"The formal opening of the day's business, when the assembled members move into the debating chamber. You won't be able to approach the PM then."

"I'll find a way of getting to him, don't worry. . . . Will there be a crowd today?"

"Yes, it's an important debate."

"Spectators?"

"Oh, by the score. But they're carefully checked."

Barry, MacBean and the plain-clothes detective were getting out of the parked car when a voice suddenly spoke from the loudspeaker on the dashboard.

"Control to Baker."

"Baker answering," said the sergeant into his microphone.

"Calling Baker Sunray."

"Sunray here." Barry was back in his seat.

"Telephone message just received," said the distant voice, sounding puzzled and scared through the distortion. "Begins 'The last one will be at two-thirty.' Ends."

MacBean had clearly heard this. He glanced up at the face of Big Ben, where the great hands pointed at 2:28, then for an instant at Barry. "Follow me," he said authoritatively, and moved away at a steady run across New Palace Yard towards the entrance to the Houses of Parliament.

"You too, Sergeant—alert Security," called Barry over his shoulder as he too began to run. "Guard the Prime Minister."

By the time Barry and the plain-clothes man had pushed through the doors and reached the foot of the broad stone stairway, MacBean was at its top, bearing left. Barry strove to keep his footing as he dodged round groups of bystanders. There were shouts behind him. He followed MacBean through a long, tall chamber thronged with people in couples and dozens and flanked at intervals with life-sized stone statues. Echoes rose and clashed and redoubled.

In the Central Lobby, when at last he reached it after a dash of a couple of hundreds of yards at his best speed, Barry shouldered his way through a mass of onlookers. He found he had lost MacBean, lost the officer who had been with him a moment before. Movements among the crowd showed that he was not the only one forcing a laborious path to its centre, to the participants in the ceremony. There was swiftly a tremendous noise, supercharged by the echoes, far too loud for any one person to make himself heard, though many were trying to. Famous faces, undistinguished faces, here and there black, brown and yellow faces, showed alarm or bewilderment or shocked apathy.

Gasping, Barry halted and looked about him in desperation. Then he caught a movement that sent him flying forward, barging aside a middle-aged woman who squawked in protest, reaching out long before he could have grabbed at what he saw. But others, two others, one in civilian clothes, the other in uniform, were there ahead of him. Between the two, a third figure struggled and was subdued and stood still. There was a great sigh, followed by a moment of silence which was Barry's chance.

"It's all over," he declared, not too loudly. "Members of the public, kindly leave the building. Police officers will show you to the exit. Members of the House, please stay where you are. There is no more danger."

By degrees, something like calm returned. Barry made explanations, promised further ones at a later time, offered reassurances, beat off the lobby correspondents who had found themselves shoved willy-nilly into contact with news material more dramatic than the most crucial debate. At last the way was clear, a screen of police formed, and the small group, with the prisoner quite unresisting at its centre, moved steadily back to the entrance and through the expectant, excited crowds that had gathered there.

CHAPTER SEVEN

Five men sat round a circular dining table in a private room at the Irving Club: Christopher Dane, Bill Barry, Peter Follett, Quintin Young, George Henderson. They had come to the cheese; the claret and the port were circulating. A coke fire crackled in the grate. Outside, the wind buffeted occasionally at the windows. Follett broke a short silence. "Poor Dickie."

"He'll get none of my sympathy," said Barry.

"Oh, come on, Bill; he couldn't help the way he was made, and but for that he'd never have had to behave as he did. He walked into an ingenious and horrible trap. I'm sure the ultimatum was delivered as late as possible, so as to give him no time to think. 'Unless you kill somebody, pin these letters to the corpse and deposit it in a certain place, I'll reveal to the authorities, not only that you're an active homosexual—names, dates and places supplied—but also that you've knowingly and deliberately helped me to commit the most atrocious series of crimes in living memory.' No use pleading that his professional integrity was as total, up to that moment, as any other man's, any more than he could hope to get away with maintaining what was just as true, that, again until that moment, he'd been an innocent, unknowing accomplice. Incidentally, did anybody realise he was that way inclined? I'd known him for twenty years and it never occurred to me."

"I'd begun to surmise it," said Young. "All that insistence on his energetic life with the ladies. Sexual boasting at every opportunity—understandable enough in youth, when you want to show you're already doing it, and in age, to show you're still doing it. But in maturity, and on that scale. . . ."

Barry made a face. "Even I wasn't quite thick enough to miss it altogether."

"Anyhow," pursued Follett, "what do you do in that situation? You can't contemplate murder even to save yourself from utter ruin, so you thump a fellow on the head as lightly as you dare, you—"

"You go straight to your Minister and make a clean breast of the whole boiling. What if that bloke Harding had had an abnormally thin skull? And what about leaving a mass murderer on the loose?"

"Of course, Bill, but all I'm saying is, I wish I could be absolutely sure I'd have done the right thing if I'd been as shocked and horrified and scared as Dickie must have been."

"I don't think I've ever seen a man more scared." Young reached for the claret. "So much so I guessed what he must have been up to that night. Well, had a hunch."

Still rather belligerently, Barry said, "And what had he got in mind for the next act in the drama? More head-bashing as required?"

"I doubt if he had anything much," said Follett. "And we'll never know now. Fortunate Dickie."

Henderson spoke into another silence. "Doubly fortunate, in a way. Men of his age often survive their first coronary."

"Trebly or triply or whatever it is fortunate," said Barry. "You may call me a rotten hard copper, but I've done more for, well, for his memory than any of you were in a position to, by closing down the Harding inquiry. Impossible if Harding had died or been seriously hurt, but as it is what we have was a crime of not all that close imitation with no leads and no economic prospect of finding any."

Henderson said, in a lighter tone than before, "I'd like to hear the whole history of this thing. I think I know the main bits and pieces, but I want them plausibly strung together. Palatably, too, if possible. And I can't think of anybody better qualified than the old master of mystery on my left."

"Thank you most kindly," said Dane, bowing in his chair. "Well, I'll tell you as much as I can, which won't be everything, because this was the sort of case that no one person could solve in its entirety. But I'll need refuelling first."

The brandy was passed to him. He took his time about pouring it and about clipping and lighting a cigar, clearly elated at the prospect of delivering the kind of discourse he had so many times put into the mouth of James Fenton. The others recharged their glasses and sat back in what was almost a parody of expectation.

"Here goes, then. It obviously started some time back, with a sense of total dissatisfaction. Fame and money weren't enough after all. I realised that that was the root of it before I knew it had even begun, or rather James Fenton did. That must have been what was really bothering me when I first talked to George and Quintin. Or is that nonsense?"

Young grinned. "Sounds like it, but a bit of crude mysticism doesn't do a writer any harm as long as he doesn't take it too seriously. Go on."

"Anyway, dissatisfaction with eminence, but also over-weening vanity. A cleverness that's real enough, but must be demonstrated to the world. Ruthlessness—you don't get far in his game without a hefty dose of that. Going with a contempt for human beings, especially those in authority. That's all there, that's given. Then something comes along and triggers it off. What it could have been. . . . Look, shall I leave out all the probablys and possiblys and tell it as a straight story?"

"That's what I meant," said Henderson.

"Okay. The story of Herostratus turned up. Just as the burning of the temple of Diana at Ephesus made the arsonist's name immortal, which was his sole motive, so some comparable act was going to keep our man's name alive long after his other achievements had been forgotten.

"What should this act be? It would have to be spectacular, clearly. And destructive. Blowing up the Houses of Parliament? Too—ordinary. Not clever enough. Assassinating the Prime Minister? Good, but it's been done before. A series of atrocious murders? Nice, but also unoriginal, and so to speak inconclusive. So combine the last two. Clever in itself, and affording scope for further cleverness: in the course of the series of murders, various clues and misdirections will be fed to the investigators which they'll be too stupid to interpret or even recognise as such. Then the final blow, delivered as publicly as possible; not only for the spectacle, but so that there can be no doubt about who was responsible for the whole affair.

"One further requirement. He must be part of the investigation, firstly to keep safely ahead of it (he mustn't be caught until he's ready), secondly, to know just what clues to feed it, and thirdly to be able to enjoy at close quarters the sight of all those high-placed fools displaying their foolishness."

With full production, Dane took a sip of brandy. "So, it might be a couple of years ago, he started preparing the ground. How could he be sure of being in on the investigation? Obviously not via the police. Then via the body with some responsibility for the police: the Ministry of Domestic Affairs. He looked about for a lever, and fate handed him a beauty—the Under-Secretary turned out to be homosexual. But that wouldn't be enough on its own; Royal's joining the inquiry had to be to some extent plausible. Hence the social conscience, the record of helping the Ministry to bring malefactors to heel, and the personal contact with Lambert-Syme.

"When the hours of darkness were approaching their longest, he started his operation. After the right interval he approached Lambert-Syme with his blackmail dossier ready for use if he should be blocked. 'What about a special inquiry team, Dickie?'—'Good idea.' Then, 'What about me being on it, Dickie?'—'Splendid notion.' And the Minister accepted it like a lamb. You remember it bothered you, Quintin: the idea that the murderer could be sure there'd be a committee and that he'd be on it. By waving his dossier, Royal could be bloody sure he'd be asked to serve as some sort of adviser to the Ministry or the police. Lambert-Syme would fix it in a twinkling."

"Without Royal having to reveal to him at that stage that he was the murderer," said Young.

"Exactly. Now for the clues and the clever trimmings. Linking the series of murders—what fun for a chap interested in crime and crime fiction. The link had to set the investigators some problem, give them some sort of disguised information. Hence the cut-out letters, which spell out HEROSTRATUS not straight but in an anagram, again just the thing for a crossword-puzzle addict, and he devised a splendidly misleading one. Too misleading: nobody seemed even to think of anagrams. I did, but no good —it was asking rather a lot to expect anyone to solve it until all the letters had appeared. Still, now we know the reason for the complete set of the previous ones with Bonello's body: that was supposed to mean, 'These have a significance over and above that of serving as a link.' I say the reason: only half the reason.

The other half was to cock a snook by fulfilling my prediction about the third factor."

"Cocking snooks is all very well," said Follett. "I understand that. But wasn't he taking a bit of a risk by fulfilling all your predictions?"

"Irresistible, as I'd hoped it would be. But he was covered by not having attended that session of the Committee and banking—rightly, I'm sorry to say—on our being too stupid to realise he could have got all the information he needed about that and subsequent sessions from someone who had attended. Most natural thing in the world that Lambert-Syme should fill him in; over the telephone would do. Another bit of snook-cocking. Not as good as the one that consisted of getting me co-opted on to the Committee, but still good. No, I went badly wrong with a vital part of my theory. You all remember me saying that the whole thing must be the work of only one individual."

Young grinned again. "That was your bum hunch, Christopher."

"I remember quite a little lecture from you on the aesthetics of power," said Follett.

"It was all right as far as it went. But I'd forgotten another very attractive form of power: over an individual. In this case, forcing a deeply law-abiding and instinctively decent man, one in authority too, to help an atrocious criminal by committing an atrocity himself. Great fun."

"But a hell of a risk, surely," said Henderson. "Dickie could easily have done as Bill said and gone straight to his Minister or the police."

"I've been thinking about it. If he'd been going to do that he'd have said so straight away—he was that kind of man. And then Royal would have killed him and gone and done the job himself. He'd have left himself time for that before his concert."

"Still a risk."

"Worth taking. He hated Lambert-Syme, you see. Right: the other clue-pattern, the points on the map that linked up to show the route between Downing Street and the House of Commons. Very sporting, all that. If somebody had worked out the Herostratus anagram (though nobody had) it would have been clear that the series was finished. If somebody had identified that route (and somebody had) there would be just enough time after that telephone call to save the PM. In fact there was. Oh, not that Royal could have visualised it the way it happened. His idea was a theoretical possibility: Bill at headquarters knowing the score, getting the call and ringing Security at the House. And of course failing to prevent the shooting even so. But the world of fools couldn't say he didn't warn it."

"Who made the 'phone-call?" asked Barry.

"Anyone. He knew dozens of people who'd have done it for a signed photograph."

"All right. What put you on to him?"

"In the first place, the fact that he proposed me for the Committee, but I can quite see that wouldn't have done for you, Bill. There were little things. Why did he mention Agatha Christie's *ABC Murders* and then say, quite irrelevantly, that he must have seen it on a news-stand?—in other words hadn't read it, knew nothing about it or crime fiction in general. But he understood *folie à deux* right off. And who knows about that apart from psychiatrists? Quintin?"

"Students of crime?"

"Thank you. And of crime fiction. One of which he'd shown himself to be by his whole line about the murderer—what was it?—'doing a thriller.' I think all that was deliberate. But a major give-away was the British Liberation Army thing. You said, Bill, quite rightly, that before they could be taken seriously they'd have to show more knowledge of the circumstances of one of the crimes than they could get from a newspaper. And they promptly knew about Pauline Hodges's birthmark. Only someone with extensive criminal contacts could have found them so fast, or at all. And that horse that got you on the hop, Peter. No gang of thugs could have thought that up. Only someone with a, what, a crime-fictional mind? What fun that must have been. Fooled again, twice over. Oh, and before anybody asks about that machine-gunning at his house, that was just a sweet, heavenly coincidence."

Follett frowned. "There've been rather too many of them in this case."

"Oh, do you think so, Peter? Too many for what? And that gunning wasn't exactly a coincidence, more like a stroke of luck. The only real coincidences have been little ones like the A-B-C of the first three surnames. None of them vital." Dane chuckled quietly to himself, shaking his head. "Anyway, it's nice to know they caught that chap Sean Whatsisname. Pretty good work in the time."

"Not really, Chris, between these four walls," said

Barry. "He got stopped by the Provisionals. Gets them a bad name, that sort of thing."

"I can see that. Well, so much for the BLA lead. I had two others—one in two parts, really. One was a question that fellows in pubs must have been asking one another all over the country, but none of us really faced. Once the reign of terror was on, how did the murderer go on inducing people to step into his parlour, his car that is, without any hesitation? With all the warnings in the Press and on television and everywhere."

"I saw one of them," Barry growled a little. "From Mr. Royal himself, done on, you know, videotape and shown just about the time he was knocking off poor Sandra Phillips. Don't have anything to do with anyone you don't know."

"Exactly. The other question concerns Sandra. Why did she lie to the police on her deathbed? Everything she said was transparent invention. The second man as an afterthought. We've come to get you, Sandra—straight out of a comic book. He had an Irish accent—all right, Peter, that was a medium-sized coincidence, but it steered us away from the truth, not towards it. As it was designed to do. Without—hats off to Sandra—running the risk of incriminating any innocent party. He must be ill. Adorable Benedict Royal must be ill in his mind to have given me a lift and then stabbed me, so I'll protect him to the end. And it's not just that they recognised him and thought he must be too nice a lad to be a mass-murderer. They felt he was a chum of theirs. Haven't we all started chatting to famous people, at parties and so on, under the unexamined impression that they must be chums of ours because their faces are so familiar? Royal didn't count as someone they didn't know.

"That's about it. Oh yes, there is the third question, how he got into the House of Commons, but they really did know him there. Visiting his friend Lambert-Syme. And oh yes, I've got a confession to make. That alibi I handed you the other day, Bill and Peter: it was a fake. Just before you arrived I realised that, like a fool I'd left myself as suspect as anyone else, and I had to get protection so as to carry you with me. I arranged it over the telephone."

"Yes, I thought it might be the telephone," said Barry.

"I didn't fool you?"

"Give me credit, Chris. I went through it out of professional curiosity. Nice job it was, both ends. No. I pretended to swallow it because there was no point in not. You couldn't be our man, because it would have meant a bloke who writes detective stories had started setting up a detective story in real life, and that kind of thing only happens in detective stories."

"Bill!" Dane sounded (and in fact was) quite shocked. "Policemen aren't supposed to think like that."

"Added to which, it's a lousy detective story where the fellow isn't caught, and you didn't strike me as the type that'd want to get caught for anything he'd done, and policemen are supposed to think like that."

"Fair enough. . . . What about Marty Mannheim? Is he in the clear?"

"Another innocent accomplice. He had to do anything Royal told him, including getting out of bed straight after a nasty shake-up, on pain of losing his job and not

getting another anywhere in the business, and Royal
gave him the impression he was off with some poof those
evenings, which Mannheim thought was likely enough,
what with Royal obviously not fancying the birds but
having to go through the motions, as you might say. The
Priest girl knew that too, better than Mannheim could,
but she came to different conclusions. Quintin, what do
you say to the idea that the whole thing started even
further back than Chris made out, with Royal so fed up
with the birds and having to go with them all the time
that he decided to get his own back on a sample of them?"

"I'd say that only rather unusual policemen are supposed to think like that, Bill. And that you're quite likely
right."

"One thing I must tell Christopher," said Follett a little
later. "Is what Royal said when we called at his place. He
sneered at me for being nowhere near catching the
criminal, and I said what I'd no right to say, that we were
closer than we had been, and he said, seeming to mean he
was doing some investigations of his own, he said, 'I bet
you're not as close to him as I am.' What about that?"

Dane uttered a small howl. "I'd give anything to have
been there. I wonder if he'd have said it if I had been
there. I believe he would. Classical indirect confession.
He had style. Too bad he had to have inhumanity,
paltriness of spirit and solipsistic egotism thrown in."

Later still, Henderson said to Young, "A pity Neil
couldn't be with us."

"Yes, it is."

Henderson looked again at his friend. "What's up?"

"I'd only tell this to another professional, George,

perhaps only to you. Neil was a patient of mine once. He's a sadist, a straightforward, old-fashioned flogger, nothing extreme. But he was worried that it might become extreme. I reassured him and sent him on his way. You can see it was a nasty shock when Dane mentioned the word in connection with Neil."

"I remember. I'd never have thought, not in a million years."

"Neither would I if he hadn't come to me. In the same way that Peter would never have guessed about Dickie. There's no art, no, repeat no art, to read the mind's construction in the face. Or anywhere else."

"*You* say that, Quintin?"

"Oh yes. And if there ever were to be such an art, we'd be safe from the Benedict Royals of this world, but we wouldn't be human any more. He's not inhuman, of course, except in terms of romantic exaggeration. I wish he were, but that's an impossibility too."

"Have some more port," said Henderson.

CHAPTER SEVEN (I)

"Take him into that room," ordered Barry, indicating a door just outside the entrance, "I'll come straight back."

He returned to the central lobby and went up to a uniformed figure on the edge of a group of people huddled near the door of the House. "Is the Prime Minister all right?"

"Oh, yes, Sir, he's gone into the chamber. The bullet hit someone else near him."

Barry turned on his heels and returned to the room where the prisoner had been taken. He recognised one or two of the officers there including the plain-clothed Inspector from the car, but went straight up to the prisoner.

"Fergus Hume MacBean, I arrest you on the charge of attempted murder. I must warn you that. . . .

"Murder? Of whom?"

"The Prime Minister. I . . . ."

"Don't be a fool, man," was MacBean's reply, "the Prime Minister is as well as you are, though he wouldn't be if it weren't for me."

"What are you trying to say?"

"Didn't you see him about to go for the Prime Minister? No, I suppose you didn't; I got ahead of you going up the stairs and I obviously know my way about here rather better than you do."

"Are you suggesting that someone else was going to attack the Prime Minister at that precise moment?"

"Exactly so, and I had a pretty good idea who it was going to be, though I must admit that I expected it to be the other one. But you're wasting time here, man, his accomplice will have got away. Police morale is low enough already and you're going to look even sillier if you waste time arresting me. How will you take a headline in the papers saying 'MP prevents assassination of Prime Minister. Arrested by police while assassin's confederate escapes'?"

"Keep him here," snapped Barry, and hurried back to the lobby and the dense group near the door of the chamber. He pushed his way towards the centre where he recognised Kemp kneeling beside a body covered with a black cloth that looked as though it were normally used for a more active ritual.

"Ah, Chief Superintendent," said Kemp as he caught sight of Barry, "I'm afraid he's dead."

"Who, for God's sake?"

"The Under-Secretary, Sir."

"Lambert-Syme?"

"Yes, Sir."

Barry took over from the Inspector and cleared the lobby of the remaining people not connected with the police. The Prime Minister had insisted on carrying on with the business of the House and those members of the Press who were undecided as to the most rewarding place to be had their minds made up for them by the formidable array of officials who had now emerged. Among these was Follett who took charge.

Some time later in one of the security offices of the House, Follett and Barry were to be found looking distinctly uncomfortable.

"I've ordered a reconvening of the Special Committee," Follett muttered, "but I'm not looking forward to it."

"At least it will keep the Press at bay for a while."

"Long enough for us to find a culprit to present to them?"

"I don't know. MacBean seemed remarkably confident. What did you make of his story?"

"It sounded more convincing than anything any of the rest of us have come up with during this damned case. And we shall look prize fools if we hold him and he turns out to be right. Dane has had his intuitions and Royal has made some hints but Lambert-Syme is the first name that has been suggested with any conviction. And a lot of the details fit very well."

Follett had spent the last hour questioning MacBean who was now at the Yard making a statement but who had made it quite clear that he expected to be released as soon as he had done so. He had been left in no doubt as

to MacBean's notion of himself as the hero who had
saved, if not the nation at least its political head and
probably its democratic institution as well.

"Let's go over his case again. He claims that he
disappeared without letting us know where he was
because he suspected that there was someone from the
Committee involved and since it might be the person
who asked everyone to keep the Committee informed of
our whereabouts he felt under no obligation to comply.
He went away with his maps and discovered that the
locations of the bodies found so far pointed towards the
Houses of Parliament as the focal point. He reckoned
that the complexity of the whole affair meant that
something big was on and the biggest thing at Westminster is the Prime Minister. Lambert-Syme had been the
person to suggest the Committee in the first place and
since so many of the subsequent events seemed to assume
a knowledge of what had gone on in the meetings of the
Committee he had reluctantly concluded that Lambert-
Syme was likely to be implicated."

"They were friends were they?"

"Well, MacBean claims that they were. They were
certainly well acquainted but I seemed to remember
Costello mentioning that he had had dinner with Mac-
Bean the night before the Committee was set up and that
when MacBean arrived he had been talking to Lambert-
Syme who went to great lengths to avoid having to meet
his fellow MP."

"MacBean had a number of other fairly plausible
supports for his theory," continued the Commissioner.
"First, there was the attack on Sandra Phillips. Allowing

for the pauses in the tape and the state she was in, it's quite possible that her phrase 'he's ill, he must be ill!' referred to the first of her attackers and there is no doubt that Lambert-Syme has both looked and, been ill just lately. He's also the only person on the Committee who fits her description of being shortish, fat, fairly old, and with grey hair."

"But Lambert-Syme was almost bald."

"Yes, but if you remember she said that he was wearing a hat and so only the hair round the edge of it would be visible. And if you don't know that someone is bald you assume the part you can't see is the same as the part that you can."

"His suggestion that her remark about a house might be another reference to the House of Commons seems a bit far fetched."

"Yes, but he conceded that himself. And one has to admit that this illness has given Lambert-Syme a good excuse for being incommunicado quite a lot of the time lately."

"Then MacBean said that he was surprised that it was Lambert-Syme who should be the one to try to assassinate the Prime Minister at a specific prearranged time since he had more or less permanent access to him and could have done it at any time he wanted; that was why he expected the accomplice to be the one who actually carried it out—so that Lambert-Syme would be in a position to influence the inevitable shake-up from his position in the Ministry."

"He could still be right there, of course. After all Lambert-Syme didn't have any gun or weapon on him so it doesn't look as though he was in fact going to do any harm to the Prime Minister."

"No, and the shot from MacBean could have frightened the real potential assassin away. The fact that MacBean was wrong in some respects doesn't mean that he isn't basically right in his conclusions. He says he was unsure as to whether the letters pinned to the bodies made a complete message or not—the second 'R' found on Colin Harding was only half a letter—but he rearranged the letters of 'south east rr' to make 'HOUSE,' 'START,' and the letter 'R.' This in combination with his findings on the map led to his deduction about the start of business at the House of Commons coupled with either a solitary 'R,' perhaps referring to Royal or an 'R' as part of another word in which case it might refer to Varga. If it was the latter he didn't think there was so much urgency since more letters would have to be found on another body first."

"Unless they were to be on the Prime Minister himself."

"Yes. He seems to have missed that possibility. He reasoned that both Royal and Varga are quite tall and thin and either could easily manage an Irish accent; indeed Varga seems to have a different accent depending on who he's talking to or what he's saying, and Royal is a professional performer. Of the two he found Royal particularly suspect because he hadn't come up with any theories of his own which was surprising for someone reputed to do *The Times* crossword in 15 minutes, and because he was known to have dealings with Lambert-Syme at the Ministry. Varga was also naturally suspect because of his well-known views on the sickness and immorality of our society which would give him a motive as well. He attributes Lambert-Syme's behaviour simply to dejection, pointing out that by the law of averages there's bound to be a spy somewhere near the seat of power and it should be as unlikely a person as possible."

"Furthermore," continued Follett, "Lambert-Syme had proposed both Royal and Varga for the Committee in the first place, thus enabling him to keep in touch with either of them without suspicion being aroused."

"And that was the state of his deliberations when we saved him the trouble of bringing them to us himself by tracking him down ourselves. Later the message about the last one being at 2:30 which he overheard in the police car confirmed his theory especially as regards the 'START' and 'HOUSE' parts. Knowing the House as well as he does he knew exactly where to find the Prime Minister. As 2:30 came up he saw Lambert-Syme going up to the Prime Minister with what he described as a strange expression on his face and putting his hand into his pocket. MacBean says that he shouted out but there was so much background noise that the PM didn't notice so he took his revolver out of his pocket and shot at Lambert-Syme, not really intending to do other than stop him. Incidentally he has a licence for the gun and claims that he has been carrying it ever since Royal was attacked. With his views on the sort of treatment that should be meted out to murderers he is showing no sign of remorse. In fact he seems to think that a proper form of justice has been done."

"And Varga and Royal?"

156   KINGSLEY AMIS

"Waiting for us at the Ministry with the rest of the Special Committee, I hope."

EXTRACT FROM THE PROCEEDINGS OF THE FINAL MEETING OF THE SPECIAL INVESTIGATORY COMMITTEE.

Present: Follett, Barry, Kemp, Paynter, Costello, Henderson, Young, Royal, Dane, Varga.

Follett: And that, gentlemen, is the line taken by MacBean. I'm sorry to put you in an embarrassing situation [here he indicated Royal and Varga especially] but as you know we have all been under suspicion to some extent.

Royal: Hence the protection?

Follett: Yes. I'm sorry to have to have used some deception there.

Varga: Deception! I hardly think you managed to deceive even this group of mindless parasites. As for the idea that any self-respecting party or country would want a flat-headed illiterate charlatan like Lambert-Syme as a defector, well, the whole idea is quite bizarre.

Barry: May I ask, all the same, Mr. Varga, where you were at 2:30 this afternoon?

Varga: If my bodyguard hasn't already told you he's about as effectual as his employers. I was at the House, of course. And a pleasant afternoon to be spent watching the Prime Minister squirm in the employment debate was entirely spoiled by that idiot MacBean. I suggest that the whole thing was set up by the Prime Minister to get sympathy and slip out of his confrontation with the trade unions.

Barry: Mr. Royal?

Royal: Do I agree? Or are you asking me if I was at the House too? Your bloodhounds will no doubt give you the lurid details of my post-prandial activities—incidentally not those I should have indulged in if they hadn't been there. No, I wasn't at the House. I can assure you I have better things to do than go and watch famous people squirming. In fact I operate on the principle of getting other people to come and see me.

Paynter: Gentlemen, somehow we are expected to confront the nation—

Varga: The nation! Rubbish! You have only got to face your own compliant lickspittle bourgeois press.

Paynter: —with a plausible solution.

Varga: (Indecipherable)

Paynter: Very well. With the truth. It would seem now the murders are at an end—

Dane: Are they?

Paynter: Mr. Dane?

Dane: Well, they would be, no doubt, if the PM had been killed, but as it is—

Paynter: Quite so. Well, all the more reason for

us to confirm MacBean's theory or else replace it. Have you any views yourself, even intuitive ones—

Dane: As some of you know I've done a certain amount of prowling of late. For what it's worth to him—and before he says it himself let me say that I don't suppose it's very much—I don't think that Mr. Varga has anything to do with it. MacBean's line is a fairly convincing one. I was intrigued to find that apart from one letter (in the Swift tradition) the "SOUTH EAST RR" message is an anagram of "ARTHUR" and "TESSA," but it seems that Arthur Johnson has been in custody since his abortive attack on Tessa Noble and she has been back at work at the Fox and Grapes. Thank goodness the SOUTH EAST part doesn't seem to have any connection with the Queen's visit to South East Asia. But I'm afraid that I haven't really come up with anything. In fact about as far as James Fenton in his latest novel, which is page one.

Paynter: Has anyone anything more concrete to suggest?

Young: Have there been any results yet to my queries about discharged psychiatric cases?

Follett: Apart from a certain Evan Williams

who we can't seem to trace there doesn't seem to be a lead there, I'm afraid.

Young: I see. Well, in common with others of you I've been worried that one of those responsible must be on this Committee—though not necessarily by design. If it is by design it looks pretty certain to me that it must have been Lambert-Syme, as Mac-Bean suggests. But my real trouble is that I can't believe that there is even one psychiatric case of the right sort among us to account for the nature of the murders, except of course for the political one this afternoon. And the idea of there being two such people here is quite unthinkable.

Paynter: And you have been in a position to observe us all quite closely.

(At this point the meeting was interrupted by a telephone call for the Commissioner.)

Follett: Follett here. You have? Where? What? You have? I'll be right over. Well, gentlemen, talking of the devil it seems that part of our search at least is over. We have discovered Evan Williams in lodgings near Euston and found enough preliminary evidence to connect him with at least some of the killings. He denies it of course but I must leave you at once to go and question him.

Varga: With the usual methods?

Paynter: Please, Mr. Varga. Yes, of course,

Commissioner. I think we should stay here. Perhaps you will let us know of any developments as soon as you can so that we can tackle the Press.

(At this point Follett and Barry left the meeting.)

Dane: (Unintelligible)

Paynter: Mr. Dane?

Dane: Of course. What idiots we've been. Quintin Young has virtually solved it for us. It all fits, and we won't even have to arrest anyone.

Young: You mean that this Williams is Lambert-Syme's accomplice?

Dane: Oh, no. Lambert-Syme was intended to be the final victim all along. And MacBean intended to kill him from the start. But he had to weave a great pattern first so that he could do it publicly without it appearing to be murder. A sort of public execution. His connection with penal matters had enabled him to single out Williams from the records as a potential accomplice and then fit his whole scheme round the particular psychotic personality at his disposal. He hated Lambert-Syme both because his position at the Ministry made him a thorn in the flesh as far as his obsession with punishment methods was concerned, and also because that position was the very one that he coveted for himself but knew he could never get. Everything in MacBean's account is consistent with his setting himself up with an opportunity to kill Lambert-Syme himself and yet still appear to be the hero of the piece. The clues he left had to be ambiguous because nobody else must be able to come to the correct conclusion about the House before him, and he had a fifteen-minute *Times* crossword man to contend with. But it still had to seem to have a pattern, and the Prime Minister had to seem to be the final target. With a combination of psychopathic killings and a political assassination who would be able to see the real motive. Moreover he had nothing to lose. I'm sure he gave that smile of his as he pulled the trigger.

Later that night, back in his house in St. John's Wood, Christopher Dane poured himself another Scotch.

"So, I was right," he said to the long-legged Rosemary, "and I didn't even need your alibi. But the idea really came from Young, and I suppose the setting up of a Committee was justified after all. Incidentally Williams fits Sandra Phillips's description of her first attacker so the taller one must have been MacBean himself. I suppose that a Lowland Scottish accent can easily be mistaken for an Irish one, especially when your mind is hardly on such things. Follett didn't have much trouble getting information out of Williams—I suppose it was an example of Young's psychopath not caring for the morrow.

But it does seem that he didn't know that his partner was MacBean, who had disguised himself at all of their meetings."

"I wonder if MacBean is pleased or sorry now there is no hanging."

"What a charming thought. Well, at least he saved me the trouble of finding a way of getting James Fenton on to page two of the new book. The Special Committee are allowing me to write the official version of the events.

"Hmm. I seem to remember you saying a couple of weeks ago that you found real murders more attractive. Still I don't see how you're going to produce your usual one a year."

"Oh, I don't know. Even if they don't invite me on to any more Special Committees at least there were enough red herrings and blind alleys in the present case for me to produce a different solution every year until MacBean is released."